SNOWS OF CRAGGMOOR

SAMANTHA HARTE

DIVERSIONBOOKS

Also by Samantha Harte

Cactus Rose

Summersea

Kiss of Gold

Autumn Blaze

Vanity Blade

Angel

Timberhill

Sweet Whispers

Hurricane Sweep

Diversion Books
A Division of Diversion Publishing Corp.
443 Park Avenue South, Suite 1008
New York, New York 10016
www.DiversionBooks.com

For more information, email info@diversionbooks.com

First Diversion Books edition March 2015.
Print ISBN: 978-1-68230-087-9
eBook ISBN: 978-1-62681-655-8

One

When I first saw the mountains from the air they looked so big! I pressed my nose against the window and stared at the monstrous crouching rocks that rose from an endless blanket of snow and pushed into leaden clouds. I wondered if the other passengers were as excited at the sight of them as I. I think we were just so tired after the three-hour delay in Denver that no one really cared where we were. At last the trip was over. For me, though, it was just the beginning—the beginning of a trip into my family's past.

A sparkling of city lights began to show through the dusk as the plane touched the icy runway. In the rush to get out of my cramped seat, I jerked my mittens on crooked and got my fingers scrambled. The passengers pressed me down the narrow aisle and suddenly I was out, standing on the wobbly stairs and sucking in stunning lungfuls of crisp mountain air. I plunged down the stairs, through the gate, and into the terminal, claimed my sorry-looking suitcase, and then headed for the only taxi in sight.

The darkness settled quickly. To me it felt colder than ever. A shiver started somewhere low in my back and crept higher and higher, like a doubt, until I was chattering and shaking with chilled resolve and cold feet.

I hesitated before waving to the taxi driver. The bitter wind whipped my hair to a froth. I jerked my stocking cap down farther over my ears. Maybe I should have stayed home after all, I thought. Yet, I'd come all this way to find out what the big family secret was. I lifted my chin and pretended I wasn't nervous. I wouldn't be going home until I knew.

Home was a little town north of Chicago. I still couldn't think about it, about Aunt Coral, or our cottage, without remembering that weird fire in the garage. I turned my face into the cold wind trying to shake off the thoughts. Sharp little snowflakes nipped at my cheeks. Nothing would ever make me forget that day two months ago—the day this journey to Colorado actually began.

"Taxi, miss?" a red-nosed man in a woolly coat called.

I nearly tripped over my numbed toes hurrying to the welcome warmth of the taxi. Don't start thinking, I told myself. Just get in and go.

"Where to?"

I snuggled back into the lumpy cushions and tried to talk over my shivers. "Craggmoor." I brushed melting snow from my shoes to hide my embarrassment over that grand, yet strange-sounding, name. I wondered if I would ever get used to it. *Me* going to some place called Craggmoor!

When the taxi didn't start moving I looked up.

"That big place up on the mountain?" he asked. His winter-blue eyes looked me over suspiciously.

"On a mountain?" I said, grinning and feeling silly.

"Yeah, I guess, if that's where Craggmoor is. Can you take me?"

"It's a long way."

I hugged my purse a little tighter. He probably figured I didn't have a dime to cross the street—and it was true, I didn't have a whole lot of money. I probably looked like a scrawny, deserted kitten after that uncomfortable nap in the Denver airport and the bumpy airplane ride. The past weeks hadn't done my face much good either. I was thinner than usual, a sorry excuse, as Aunt Coral used to tease. "I'm in no hurry," I said, smiling hopefully at the driver.

He turned and covered his chuckle. Soon he was winding his way out to the highway. We followed a snowplow into the city and then headed south toward the dark, looming mountains.

I liked Colorado Springs right away. The streets stretched wide and straight. Victorian houses and stately pines lined them, looking something like etchings in a history book. "I'll bet some of these places date back to gold rush days," I said, craning my neck to see everything.

"Yep, so does Craggmoor."

At least I knew that much. Why hadn't Aunt Coral ever told me about the place? All my life I had thought she and I were the only Glendens left in our family. Then last September, just after I'd started back to classes at the art institute in Chicago...

It had been one of our usual mornings together. Aunt Coral sat on the sofa doing needlepoint under her magnifying glass and watching the earliest game show on TV. I was hurrying to catch the train into the city, late as usual. "Come on," I had said, racing around, reaching for a sweater, gathering up drawings. "You've got a doctor's appointment in fifteen minutes. I'll walk you over to the clinic. If you miss again, Doc Hayes will probably send out a search party."

"Bother that old quack," Aunt Coral had huffed, viciously jabbing her needle into the canvas. "He thinks a hospital bed and lots of bills is just what I need. No, Merri, I'm going to stay right here. I've got lots to do today. I'll thank you to be on your way. I expect great things of you."

It was useless to argue with her. She and I both had hard spots in our heads and there was no getting through to us sometimes. She thought going to art school was a waste of time. I should be out husband hunting. Since I wanted to become a commercial artist someday though, she helped me with the tuition and clucked over my sketches and generally expected "great things."

I jumped when the taxi driver called back to me, "Warm enough for you back there?"

"Fine!" It seemed like all I did any more was daydream. I settled back and pulled my coat tighter. The memories kept coming. That last hot September afternoon seemed like only hours ago. Sooner or later I would have to think it all out. Shuddering, I finally let myself remember.

The commuter train I rode home from school had been crowded that day. I was glad to get off and start the quiet walk home through puddles of orange and red leaves. I was thinking of a painting I wanted to do and was wondering if I still had enough oils to work with. The classes had left me little time to paint. I was itching to spread some color around. Mentally I sketched a landscape and imagined the golds and russets I would use on the trees. When I saw a curl of smoke just over the hill I sniffed the breeze for the scent of burning leaves. The smell made me faintly sick. Suddenly a puff of black, oily smoke smudged the sky from the direction of Aunt Coral's cottage. I was running even before I realized that it was our own incredibly ancient garage that was on fire.

A siren already cried in the distance as I reached the gate and raced down the crooked stone path to the garage's back door. It was locked. "Aunt Coral!" I screamed. "Are you in there?" I pounded and pounded. Through the rain-spotted window, I saw her lying beside piles of old clothes. Her favorite camelback trunk was belching out great gobs of black smoke.

Grabbing the nearest flowerpot, I smashed the window. Only a worn slide bolt latched the door. I reached it and burst inside. "Get up!" I kept yelling.

The fire truck stopped in the road. Half a dozen men pushed me out of the way. I wound up outside standing in the fading bed of marigolds while they did all the work. All I could do was cry. "What's she doing in there?" I asked as they carried her out and laid her in the grass. I knelt beside her and kept patting her wrist.

It wasn't until the big fans were blowing all the smoke away that they started to listen to my question. "What *was* she doing in there? She just about set herself on fire burning trash inside like that!" the firemen shouted.

Aunt Coral trying to burn the treasures in her trunk? I couldn't believe it. She loved all those old things. She kept love letters, satin party dresses, cracked and yellowed kid gloves, crinolines, family albums…Someone else must have set the fire, I decided. She had been trying to put it out.

"Look at this mess," the firemen said.

I looked up. One of them was holding a box of matches just like the ones in our kitchen. Matches? She *did* set the fire herself! Why? "What were you doing in there?" I said turning back to her. I stroked her velvety soft cheek and rubbed at my own tears. "Why would you want to burn things you've saved all your life?"

Her eyes fluttered. She smiled ever so slightly and then her head lolled on my arm.

Aunt Coral used to show me the albums she loved so much. She made great ceremony of opening the trunk's awkward latches and lifting the heavy lid. In all the years I had lived with her, I treasured those special times when we sat together in the garden and looked at the pictures of my father and mother, and old fiery-eyed Grandpa Davy. But whenever I tried to see what else she kept in the trunk, she would say, "You're a good girl, Merri, and I love you dearly— but these things are mine. You mustn't ever get into them."

I never asked why. Aunt Coral shared everything with me except those secret things. The fact that she *had* secret things made her special and even more wonderful.

"We'll have to take her now," the ambulance driver said, prying me loose.

"But why?" I asked, stumbling out of the way. "Why her treasures?" I no longer cared that those things lying in the blackened, waterlogged trunk were her secrets. I wanted to know why she had tried to burn them. What had been so important?

"Wait," I cried as the ambulance started to pull away. "I have to go with her."

The captain held me back. "It's no use, Merri," he

said softly, as if I were a child who might not be able to understand what he was going to say. "She didn't make it. She wasn't very strong. Did she have a weak heart?"

I pressed my hands against my mouth to hold back the sobs. They came anyway. Yes, I thought. She was old and had worked hard all her life. I had been too soft on her. I should have insisted...

"The smoke..." He tried to explain. "Guess we'll never know what she was trying to hide. Don't you worry now. My sister's got a rooming house right up the street. Why don't you move in there...until the funeral is over? You don't want to be alone just now."

Alone. It was a crushing, sinking feeling that settled around me after the ambulance and fire trucks were gone. It stayed with me over the next few days. And when it was all over I felt haunted. Why? Always, why? After a time I went through the things she had taken out of the trunk. I couldn't see much meaning in old dresses and fragile teacups or hand-embroidered linens mildewed with time.

She had heaped only old letters and newspapers into the trunk and set fire to them. Finally one afternoon I settled down to go through the ashes bit by bit. Almost everything was hopelessly blackened. The rest was stuck together from the water.

Only when I got to the bottom did I find pieces big enough to read. Under a 1930s fashion magazine I found a brown manila envelope full of letters. I settled back on my heels.

Each letter was addressed to my grandfather. All I knew about Grandpa Davy was that he had died just before I was born. He had married late. My dad and Aunt Coral had been born when he was over fifty. Aunt Coral had been my only family. Grandma Glenden died too, when I was too little to remember her—and there were my folks...

Here was somebody named George Glenden who had written a lot of letters to Grandad back when he must have been only thirty or forty. Had Aunt Coral been trying to keep me from learning about that? I certainly didn't care what happened that long ago. I wasn't interested in reading them now that she was gone, either. She should have known me better. I slid the letters back into the envelope without opening even one. I was curious, but if it mattered that much to her...

A worn, brown photo fell into my lap. It was of a beautiful woman taken long ago. Her name, grown faint over the years, was scrawled across the back. To me it looked like it said Merrisa Glenden. My name!

I forgot everything. I wanted to know who she was. I opened the letters and began to read. "David, you must write soon. Father will never change his mind if you don't. You can't turn your back on us. How can you change what you are?"

"David, our mother isn't well. You can't be so cruel. She needs you. You were always her favorite."

"David, why don't you write? Father's solicitor confirmed your address. You're receiving my letters. Couldn't you have at least come to the funeral? We would have sent passage."

The last letter had been ripped to bits and then painstakingly pieced back together with now-brittle cellophane tape. I sensed the insult intended in every overly polite word as it began to fall apart in my hands. No wonder Grandad stayed away. And yet...

I still didn't see what was so terribly important about the letters that Aunt Coral had to burn them. Then, under an edge of the trunk's lining paper on the very bottom, I found the yellowed newspaper clipping. Aunt Coral had written the date in the margin eighteen years before, when I was about two.

It was a picture of a child and her family under a gigantic, glittering Christmas tree. The splotchy printing at the bottom read: Stewart Glenden and his new wife, Natalie, of Craggmoor, Colorado Springs, built in 1887 by mining tycoon Clinton Glenden, celebrate Christmas with their children. Pretty little Merrisa accepts the heirloom German nativity to...The rest was torn off.

Merrisa! My name again! Could it be that I was the great-granddaughter of a tycoon? I shook off that crazy idea as soon as I thought it. The little girl was about my same age at the time. It was my name—but she had dark hair and clear, crystal-colored eyes. My hair had always been fair and my eyes dark like my mother's. That wasn't me!

I had a cousin! And not just an ordinary one. She had my name. She was nearly my age—we would be more like twins. I was so excited I wrote to her at Craggmoor that day. While I waited for her to write back I settled Aunt Coral's property. I rented out the cottage and got a room at the rooming house. A week later, after hearing nothing from cousin Merrisa, I wrote again explaining about my new address. I knew I sounded crazy claiming to be her cousin and having the same name, but I had an itch to know what my aunt had been hiding all those years. My cousin was the key.

Three weeks went by and still I heard nothing. I felt lonely and discouraged and depressed. I couldn't go back to art school. I used Aunt Coral's savings for the funeral. I had no prospects for a job. Most of my friends worked or were away at college. I'd pinned my hopes on finding my cousin. And she didn't even bother to answer.

I wrote once more. I had about given up when the letter came back unopened—stamped Addressee Unknown.

Anything could have happened to her, I told myself. She could have moved. Maybe Craggmoor was gone. Mrs. Evans, who ran the rooming house, suggested I call. "Call who?" I laughed. "My cousin? Hi, Merrisa, this is Merrisa, you don't know me, but…"

"You'll never know until you try," she said, sounding just like Aunt Coral.

"The letter came back, though. She's not there any more."

"If she's young like you, she could be at college. Or maybe vacationing on the Riviera."

I laughed. "Craggmoor does sound like a mansion or something, doesn't it?"

So I tried. After several calls, I could only locate the secretary of the estate's attorney. The operator was probably as glad as I was that I got that much. I explained that I wanted to talk to whoever still lived at Craggmoor. "I'm a relative." I laughed, feeling as nervous as if I were making a crank call. "I'd like to let someone know where I am—my name is Merri Glenden."

A long, embarrassing pause made me want to give up and forget the whole thing. "One moment," she said, moments later. "Miss Glenden? I have that number for you. Be sure to speak to Stewart."

I'll never forget the conversation that followed. I had rehearsed how I would introduce myself. It was so confusing to explain about my name and what I wanted—which I wasn't sure of myself. And who was Stewart? With my voice as weak and trembly as if I were reading a speech at school, I called Craggmoor and asked for Stewart.

A tired-sounding man answered.

"Hi, I'm Merri Glenden," I said excitedly. "I'm not who you think I..."

"Merry!" He sputtered so much he couldn't say anything more!

All thoughts flew from my head. Laughing hesitantly, I started again. "My name is Merrisa. My grandfather was David. His father was Clinton..."

"Merry! Merry, baby! Where are you?"

"Huh? I'm calling from Illinois."

"Please come home. Don't do this to your daddy."

"You're not...I'm not..." I got so upset I wanted to hang up. "Please," I said. "I'm not who you think I am. We're getting mixed up!"

The man started crying! "I don't know why you left, honey. I don't care. If it was Rosinna again, forget about her. If it was me—please—don't hold things against me. I'm not strong like you want. Just come home. Your daddy needs you."

His words tore at my heart. Where was my cousin? It sounded like he didn't know!

"Baby, please."

"If I could just explain..." I said.

"Just come home, Merry. You'll see. I'll get better. As long as you're here..."

And, there I was. I was never able to explain that I was just a distant cousin, not his daughter. When I hung up I felt terrible. He was as lonely and miserable as I. Didn't he have anyone else? Where had Merrisa gone—and why?

I had made and canceled several reservations before I finally got up the nerve really to go out to Colorado and meet this man who was my cousin's father. Why not? I asked myself. I had a little money. I wasn't busy. And I did want to know why Aunt Coral had tried to keep me from learning that I had other family.

What I didn't realize was that nobody knew what had happened to Merrisa Glenden of Craggmoor—my mysterious cousin. In going there I was about to stir up something more awful than I could have ever imagined.

Just as the taxi reached the mountains jutting up in a snowy jumble of rock and pine, the driver stopped.

"Is this it?" I asked, leaning forward to see ahead.

"Almost. Thought you'd like to see Craggmoor before we get up to it. The main building is too far back to see from the road."

Scanning the mountain's face, I suddenly saw where he was pointing. A wall of stone made me think of a medieval fortress.

"They say there's a great view," the driver said. "Had tours one summer. My wife went. Funny, you don't look like a jet-setter."

I giggled. "Just a distant cousin."

"Here to meet your old Aunt Matilda and inherit her millions, right?" he snorted.

He started up again. The well-plowed road coursed up

the mountainside. Everything was so beautiful. My hands itched for pencil and sketch pad. He could have stopped anywhere and I would have been satisfied to sit and draw for hours.

At last he turned down a snow-choked cut in the pines. After a quarter of a mile we stopped in a silent expanse of untouched snow. The taxi crunched to a stop.

"What's this?"

"The parking lot. Guess they don't even plow any more. Well, this is it—the gate to Craggmoor. Good luck."

My eyes shot to the towering iron gate at the far side of the lot. Lions topped the stone pillars on either side. I had a tiny link with this?

I leaped from the taxi, dragging my suitcase after me. I paid the driver and stood waving as he made a wide circle and drove away. The iron words arching over the gate became legible as I got closer: CRAGGMOOR.

I imagined how long ago enameled carriages and rich, gallant men of the West, wearing thick silver buckles, entered Craggmoor through that gate. I hardly felt the weight of my suitcase or the snow in my shoes as I hurried closer. What a place!

I was so excited I didn't notice at first when the quiet closed around me. Only the pines whispered and bent to the wind. It was a little frightening. As I crept nearer, my heart suddenly began to thud. I looked over my shoulder and my back twitched.

I could hardly see the taxi's tire tracks from that distance. Only my crooked footprints marked the snow. I felt as though I had crossed more than a parking lot. Time and my old life and all that I had known before fell behind me in frozen suspension. I was alone. I would never be quite the same after coming to Craggmoor. And that, perhaps more than anything, was what Aunt Coral had known would happen if I found this place.

At the gate I set my suitcase down and tugged at a barred doorway. It creaked and clattered, locked with a bolt set deep in the pillar.

When I saw the intercom I chipped the ice away and pressed the button. I rang again and waited.

"Is someone there?" came a woman's frosty voice over the speaker. "Who's there?"

"Merri Glenden," I shouted. I didn't worry about being mistaken that time. I wanted to be. The cold cut right through my coat and I was ready for someplace warm and snug.

I expected some kind of reply, but heard nothing. Suddenly the bolt sprang back. The gate swung open as if a ghostly hand held it. Ahead lay a wide snowy drive as inviting as an old-fashioned Christmas card.

I grabbed my suitcase and hurried through. The gate shuddered closed and the bolt made a loud *clunck* as it fell back into place. I took a deep breath and swallowed. Here I go, I said to myself.

Even though the snow was a foot deep, the knee-high white-capped shrubs neatly outlined the way ahead. Another narrow path disappeared between pines on my left. I could see some of the city and the snow-dotted plains stretching to the horizon. In the distance a plane headed for the airport.

Rounding the curve, I stopped. There was Craggmoor! I couldn't believe it. I'd expected a house, a grand house of course, large and dignified—but nevertheless a house. Before me, however, stood a strange place. It was built of massive stone squares. Rows upon rows of barred windows loomed in the eerie darkness—and none of them showed any light. Gargoyle carvings decorated the face of it. Lightning rods spiked the roof. Craggmoor was so large the back left off somewhere in the pines. It reminded me of a museum— closed and deserted. The wind picked up and began to cry, as if warning me to be quiet, to be careful, to be just a bit more scared than I was.

I stumbled over the curb to the sidewalk, which turned toward Craggmoor and divided, circling a frozen fountain, complete with ugly marble cherubs. I followed it to a sweep of treacherous icy terraced steps.

Beyond a rocky wall to the right a small pond reflected the darkening slate-gray sky. Formal gardens to the left were still beautiful even in the dark and blanketed with snow.

I looked back over my uncertain trail. Past the fountain and drive, the yard dropped off at a hedgelined wall. A huge, semicircular lawn eased out beyond the trees to overlook the panoramic view of the city. Spruce lined the path along the wall supported by the formidable stone face I had seen from below.

Something moved behind me. I spun around. A woman stood in the open front doorway. She looked small in proportion to it. I tried to smile.

"What do you want?" she demanded. Her critical gaze swept over me and settled with surprise on my suitcase.

"My name is Merri Glenden," I said. "I'm a cousin of the Merrisa Glenden you know. I wrote, but..."

"She no longer lives here," the woman answered flatly. She stared at me with cold, level eyes, the same malevolent gray as the stormy sky.

My face went red and my hands went cold. The wind whipped my hair and I shivered. "I—I spoke to Merrisa's father just last week. He thought I was she, I mean my cousin. I came to straighten things out." That sounded dumb, even to me. "Since I never heard of this place before I was a little curious, too."

"Curious about what?"

"My cousin Merrisa. We have the same name! Is she really missing?"

She pulled the door partially closed behind her. Hugging her sweater more closely, she fixed a stern eye on me. "You said your name was what?"

"Merri—Merrisa Glenden. I'm from Illinois. My Aunt Coral had papers my grandfather left her. That's how I found out about my cousin who has the same…There's a newspaper clipping of her. I was…curious."

She glared at me, hoping to scare me away probably. I looked her over too. She wore a tailored navy-blue dress so crisp it had to be new. Her navy-tinted stockings and matching shoes made a perfect ensemble. Her hair was dark, combed in a simple style that looked like it had just been done. She made me feel scruffy.

Uncertainly, I edged back, ready to give up. Then I remembered that locked iron gate. "I guess if she's not here…I just thought…I'll go now if you'll let me out."

"I think you're an impostor," she snapped.

I jumped. "I really am Merri Glenden!"

"Perhaps, but you're not related to any of us."

"Don't you think it's kind of funny I have the exact same name and that she and I are about the same age? That's why I came, because it's so strange."

"Strange that you should travel all this way uninvited? I think yes."

"I wrote!"

"You don't expect me to fall for this peculiar story of yours, do you?" She smiled condescendingly.

"No, I guess you wouldn't." I sighed, half turning. "But it was fun, thinking I had a cousin who…"

"You cannot fool me, young woman! You are *not* a cousin. Now, get off this property before I call the police."

My tears were dangerously close. "Maybe you don't believe it, but it's true."

"What do you hope to gain by this cheap trick?" she demanded.

I glimpsed something in her eyes then that puzzled me. I was no detective, but I'd studied art and had drawn lots of faces. I had learned something about expressions—and eyes. In hers, I saw fear.

What had happened to Merrisa, my mysterious cousin?

I straightened and looked at her squarely. "I wanted to meet her. I wanted to know if she was anything like me."

"Who sent you here?" The woman's voice was trembling just a little.

"Nobody. I came all by myself. My aunt died two months ago trying to get rid of my grandfather's papers just so I wouldn't find out about this place. I wondered why. Now I guess I know."

"I fail to see how you can claim kinship with this old and established household," she retorted haughtily. "We have no other branches of the family. We are the only ones."

"There is me!" I shot back. "My grandfather was David Glenden. I don't know exactly when he left the family, but I could give a good guess."

She sighed impatiently, edging back into the doorway.

I shuddered. I'd been a fool to think they'd welcome me, a stranger, a poor relation with a flimsy story. It was just like that taxi driver thought, that I was after money.

Suddenly though, the heartbreakingly sad voice of the man on the phone came back to me—the man I had wanted to meet. I couldn't leave without saying hello to him. So I hung there, impatient to get away and yet wishing I could stay.

"David—David," she mumbled, as if trying to place the name. Suddenly she took a step forward. "One moment, Miss...Glenden. Where did you get our name? Out of *Who's Who?*"

"Huh? No! He was my grandfather. I'll bet his mother's name was Merrisa. I'm named for her—the same as my cousin. I even have her picture."

"Indeed?"

"Can I show you? I don't want you to think this is a trick. I really am Merri Glenden. I don't want money or anything. I just wanted to see my cousin. I've gone through my whole life thinking I was the only Merrisa Glenden in the world. Finding another one, the same age, is special."

"Show me then. Show me the picture you claim to have."

I fumbled with the zipper pocket of my suitcase. My fingers were cold and stiff. Finally I got the envelope out and handed her the faded photo of my great grandmother.

She studied it. She squinted almost angrily at the blurred name on the back. Then she raised puzzled eyes. I knew she was beginning to believe me.

"I have letters—and the newspaper clipping! Aunt Coral

kept it locked in the bottom of her trunk for eighteen years. Imagine that? Eighteen years and she never told me!"

I watched excitedly as she read the letters. She gasped a little at the newspaper clipping, as if she'd seen it before herself.

"Then you didn't know Merry was gone when you wrote those three letters?" she mumbled.

"I never heard of Craggmoor before." I ventured a bit closer. "You mean you got my letters?"

"They arrived."

She read everything again and studied the photo as a suspicious jeweler might examine a diamond.

"I suppose all this can be verified?" she asked, raising a quizzical eyebrow.

"Verified?" I asked, feeling my cheeks flush.

"Birth and death records of these people you claim existed?"

"I guess so."

"Whatever was Uncle David doing in Illinois? I know of this man—my great-uncle, I believe. Black sheep of the Glendens. Did you know him?"

"He died before I was born. My father was a farmer. He and my mother died in a tornado when I was seven."

"A farmer." She sniffed.

I bristled. Anybody that suspicious had to have something to hide. She probably knew where Merry was and just wasn't saying.

"Very well." She sighed, returning the papers. "Forgive me for keeping you in the cold but you must understand my position. You *are* a stranger. This household is rather my responsibility. Please, do come in and have some tea. I must say, your letters caused quite an uproar. I returned the last one, to *end* them, hopefully. Then your call...Stewart is not strong. It upset him terribly. I've managed to convince him our Merry isn't coming back. Who *you* were, however, was beyond us all."

"I'm sorry," I said, reaching stiffly for my suitcase. "I meant no harm."

She nodded, her eyes still impersonal and expressionless. Standing aside, she pushed the ornate door open and I went in.

It closed behind me, giving me the feeling that the last link with the outside had been cut. We walked down the wide, white-tiled entrance hall, our footsteps clicking loudly. Mahogany doors and a broad, dark banister contrasted with pale creams and blues. It was a cool, dignified place and I think I could have liked it if there had been a single smile among the portraits hanging all around me.

She led me past the magnificent staircase toward the back. "We spend our time in the servants' quarters during the winter," she explained. "This larger portion is impossible to heat, as you can imagine."

We entered the country kitchen. Servants' quarters, were they? She could have fooled me. The rooms were fancier than anything I had ever seen.

"You see," she went on, subtly drawing my attention to rows of cabinets and overhead racks crowded with copper pots, and leading me to a comfortable side room. "There isn't anything so mysterious about Merrisa, except that, of course, her disappearance caused Stewart so much anguish. Merrisa isn't missing. She's just gone."

I put my suitcase down.

"Another black sheep, I fear." She smiled icily. "Streaks of rebelliousness run through most families, I suppose. Ours is no exception. David turned his back on the wealth his father Clinton built—couldn't handle the responsibility, though it would have all been his. He and my grandfather George were bitter rivals. That, however, was a personal matter. I'm not aware of the details. Merrisa, too, decided the wealthy life was not for her. She left two years ago when she was nineteen."

"Somehow I hadn't imagined it that long," I said.

"Please, let me take your coat."

She tossed it gingerly over her arm and rang a little silver bell on her way out. Moments later a plump lady brought a china tea service. The cups were edged in gold. The palest of pale pink roses floated around the graceful teapot like clouds on faintly mint-colored leaves. Everything was so lovely, I felt stunned.

The room was large and warm, richly paneled and muted by a soft gold carpet. Most of the furniture was old-fashioned, upholstered in what I recognized right away as antique petit point. Aunt Coral would have adored it!

Gleaming, fine-grained tables and elaborate lamps gave the room a cozy glow. I headed right for the fireplace and, while my body thawed, I gazed in wonder at the landscape hung over the marble mantelpiece.

"Do you appreciate art?" the woman asked, returning.

"I was in art school until...Aunt Coral died."

She sat down on a luscious divan and poured the tea. I took a seat across from her. Handing me a lacy napkin, she smiled quite nicely.

"I don't believe I've properly introduced myself," she

said. She sat perfectly straight with her knees clamped together, almost like a paper doll.

She was attractive, I decided. She had to be the way she was dressed. She was too thin though. Her chin looked as if it had been chiseled from some of Craggmoor's granite.

Her hand trembled when she lifted her teacup. "My name is Rosinna Glenden," she said. Pride improved her voice. "I'm Merry's half-sister. Stewart is our father. My mother was Germaine, who came to Colorado from Boston years ago. I also have a brother who lives here. His name is Jerome. After our mother died, Stewart remarried and along came Merrisa, the baby of the family."

Then she raised her eyebrows and went on sipping. It was my turn.

"I was raised by Aunt Coral," I said. "That's all the story I've got."

"This is extraordinary." She smiled. "I'm sure Merrisa would have loved to meet you. I'll keep in touch after you leave. Perhaps someday the two of you will meet."

"I hope so."

"I'm sorry your trip was a waste."

"If only…" I shook it off and gave up the idea of asking her more about my cousin. It obviously wasn't my business.

"I'd love to see the grounds in summer," I said instead.

"Yes, Craggmoor's best then. It takes a veritable army of gardeners to keep them up. I do love it so; it seems worth the expense. Nowadays grand mansions are not appreciated." She almost blushed. Color made her look more human. "I have an ambition to restore Craggmoor to its former elegance," she went on, gazing into her teacup. "Many of the rooms have been neglected. Without guests, there really is no need to keep them up." She paused. The lapse grew longer and longer. "I am curious. If you knew your cousin wasn't here, why did you come at all?"

"I upset Mr. Glenden...I thought..." I shrugged.

"We do all we can for him. He's ill, you see. That's why we live so simply. Someday when Father is well again we'll live as we did when Mother was alive. She knew how to handle a busy household. Ah, the parties she gave, the dignitaries who once stayed upstairs!"

"I heard you used to have tours."

She stiffened visibly. "Unfortunately yes, a few years ago we opened the doors to gawkers and pocket thieves. Merry's idea," she said with distaste. "My hope is, however, to live here fully with the frequent, prominent guests my mother once enjoyed. I want to bring back the elegance of past years. But then, you're not interested in my frivolous ideas."

"It sounds great!"

She smiled wanly. "I fear my hopes are only that. The estate is frozen. Stewart turned it over to his attorney when he was ill two years ago. A substantial part was put in Merrisa's name. Then, after Stewart's partial recovery, she disappeared. Until she is found, or the statute of limitations runs out, I will be powerless to improve, or even maintain, the estate. Jerome's portion of it along with mine is not adequate." Her eyes snapped. Then suddenly she veiled them.

Had Merry just left, I wondered, or had this ruthless, older half-sister forced her away?

"I wish I could help you find Merry somehow," I said when the silence grew long and uncomfortable.

She looked quite surprised. "Do you?"

"Well..." I shrugged. "Somebody should look for her."

"I assure you, we have done everything possible. When her suitcase was discovered gone, along with certain belongings, we had to accept the fact that she ran away."

"Like Grandad."

"As I said, Merry was dissatisfied with our sedate life. She was a spirited girl, given to mild tantrums and rebellions. She wanted her own way and wanted people to behave as she wished."

"Could I follow her?"

She chuckled. "Hardly. We do employ a rather expensive detective. He's turned not a clue. Garth keeps him on regardless. Unlike us, Garth has use of the estate money. In the meantime we…" She pursed her lips with annoyance.

"I should have guessed you'd have her followed. You must think I'm awfully dumb."

"Oh, no." She dabbed her lips with the napkin. "You are straightforward, but not obnoxiously so. Merry, on the other hand, was quite spoiled and brazen."

"Brazen I'm not." I laughed.

Rosinna paused to consider that. Then she went on. "Merry would have found a name-sister quite intriguing and romantic, I think. Pity she's not here. She'd take you skiing, no doubt."

The tea was gone. I knew it was time to leave. We chatted as I wrote my address, thinking in the back of my mind that she'd probably "verify" it, too.

She ushered me so skillfully to the front door I forgot all about seeing Stewart Glenden or my desire to sketch. I followed her without a word of protest.

"Just reach through the bars when you get to the gate. Press the button and I'll open it for you. It was so nice meeting you, Merri. *Do* keep in touch. I'll let you know if I ever hear from my sister."

She offered her hand and I shook it awkwardly. Her grip was firm and cold, her smile carved in stone. As she opened the door a gust of wind nearly wrenched it from her hands. Snow swirled into the hall.

"Do be careful driving!" she exclaimed as I ducked out. "And Merri, just to ease any concern you may have about your cousin—I feel I should admit I know a little more about it than I've let on—to the police at any rate. Reputations must be preserved, you understand. Family matters kept private."

I turned, nearly blinded by the swirling snow. "Then you do know where she is?"

"No. I only know she ran away to get married. The young man was quite unsuitable. We all forbade the match, but Merry was headstrong. She insisted. Please, this *is* in confidence."

Bewildered and amazed, I nodded.

"Good-bye then." She smiled uncertainly.

The door closed. There I was, swathed in stinging snow. The cold seemed to drive right through to my skin. What was I going to do now? Rosinna had assumed I'd driven to Craggmoor. How would I get back to town?

She was so strange. I didn't want to get mixed up with her, or anyone else in her family. If it hadn't been so cold and dark I would have been glad to be out of there.

I started down the steps, hidden in drifting snow by then. I made it almost to the bottom before I fell.

Two

With one careless step, my feet went out from under me. It wasn't a bad fall. I didn't get hurt, but the snow sifted down inside my collar. I hopped up to shake it out, gasping with cold.

I was brushing off my coat when I heard heavy footsteps coming up the drive. A tall man ran around the curve, his head bent against the wind. He plowed into me without ever looking up. I almost fell down again.

"I'm sorry!" he exclaimed, as we steadied each other.

At last, a pleasant face, I thought as a little shiver of excitement went through me. He looked delicious in wool. The fur collar of his coat nearly matched his full brown hair. Except for a pair of snapping blue eyes, he had the most attractive, square-jawed face I'd ever seen. He smiled and I found myself smiling back.

"Who are you?" he said, laughing.

"My name is"—snow nearly swept my words away— "Merri Glenden. I've explained *that* so many times now I'm just worn out!"

"You're not leaving?"

"It looks that way."

"Didn't Rosinna let you in? I know she's in there."

"She was very suspicious at first. After I convinced her I wasn't after her millions we had a pretty nice talk."

"Rosinna put you out in this storm? Traveler's warnings are out. I can't believe it! Rosinna keeps herself so isolated here she wouldn't know if the world decided to quietly sneak away." He chuckled. "Don't mind me. Is that your suitcase?"

I nodded—and my cap blew off.

He chased and caught it. Gingerly he slipped it back over my hair. When his gloved hand touched my cheek I felt like the sun had momentarily passed close by. "What brings you here?" he asked, flashing that inviting smile again.

"My cousin. I just found out about her. Obviously no one here knew about me." I explained briefly where I was from and how I came to be at Craggmoor.

"Fantastic!" He laughed, seizing my suitcase and guiding me up the icy steps.

"My aunt was a terrific lady," I went on. "I still don't know why she hid everything from me. This is all"—I waved my hands to indicate the house and grounds—"something to be proud of. I'm so excited—well, I was. Rosinna made me feel like I was just as well off never having come. I'd hoped to meet cousin Merry."

"You say your aunt knew all these years?" the man said, looking so closely at me my cheeks began to burn.

I described the fire in the garage. "If I'd been any later even the letters would have been destroyed. When Rosinna told me that Merry ran away to get married I—"

"Wait a minute!" He pulled me up short at the door. "Rosinna told you she got married?"

I met his blazing blue eyes reluctantly. Inwardly I groaned. "She told me in confidence. I've got such a big mouth!" I shrugged and made a helpless little smile. "I assumed you knew."

He looked away, wheels turning behind those eyes. I realized I had no idea who he was. Uneasily I stepped backward, longing for the safety of the darkness beyond the gate.

"She neglected to tell me that small detail," he grumbled.

"Maybe you'd better tell me who you are." I sighed. "I don't know anybody here and yet every time I turn around I've got my foot into something. That lady is going to be awfully angry. I told a secret in five minutes that she's managed to keep for two years."

His eyebrows lifted and his shoulders relaxed. "I'm Garth Favor; attorney, handyman, what-have-you. I also have the dubious distinction of being a member of the family."

"Oh!" I said, recognizing the name. Then my face fell. "Oh." Member of the family? Cousin, brother, husband? It was silly to feel disappointed, but...

He grinned and cocked his head. His eyes began to twinkle with amusement. "Rosinna told me"—he went on as if he hadn't just read my mind—"that Merry left to escape the rich decadence of our life."

A smile tugged at my pout. "Maybe she was just trying to satisfy my curiosity," I said. "She talked about reputations and all that. She probably just wanted me to go away and made the whole thing up."

"Rosinna is a perfectionist when it comes to appearances.

Never a more proper lady—a walking book on etiquette. She cringes at the thought of public scandal. When the police had their investigation after Merry disappeared it nearly drove her up the wall! Our detective hasn't turned up anything in two years either. You're the only clue we've found, and that doesn't count because you discovered us. Now this 'little discrepancy.' How interesting, I say. Rosinna has made a glaring boo-boo. I'm quite surprised."

With Merry only nineteen years old and holding the biggest portion of the family money, just why *did* she leave? What was Rosinna hiding?

"What's wrong?" he asked. He'd lifted my suitcase again. There were lots of square-shaped holes in the snow that followed our trail to the door. I felt as if I had known Garth Favor for years and immediately found myself at ease and confessing my growing suspicions. "What really happened to Merry? Why did she leave, really?"

He flapped his arms and made an annoyed face. "Who knows about anybody around here?" He shook a fist. "Rosinna!" Then he threw his arm around my shoulder. "She's about as friendly as a mountain lion. You're probably dying to go home to Illinois and resume a nice normal life— but I'm willing to stipulate that you were hoping to stay. I didn't see a car out in the lot. Tire tracks from a weary but rich taxi—yes. Expensive from town, isn't it?" He grinned. I wasn't sure I liked having him read me so easily.

"I really didn't have much in mind," I said lamely.

"Rosinna called you a cab then?"

"She let me out before I could explain…"

He looked impatient. "Then, come in again. We have a lot to talk about. I want to hear more of your story, naturally.

You might be interested in some of the questions I plan to put to Rosinna. Want to stay and watch the fireworks?"

He banged the lion's-head doorknocker until the door shuddered.

After a long wait Rosinna flung the door wide. "Garth!" She said it like an oath. "What are you doing…" Seeing me, a flash of confusion and irritation crossed her face. She recovered with a smile. "I thought *you 'd* gone."

"You mean, you hoped," Garth muttered, pushing his way inside. He dropped my suitcase on the floor and leveled brimstone eyes on Rosinna. "I thought you had impeccable manners, but to let a visitor leave in a blizzard like this…It's criminal. Come on, Merri. You look frozen."

Rosinna huffed angrily and turned just enough so I couldn't see how narrow her eyes were. I smiled helplessly and edged in. What was I going to do now? I wished I *could* go back to Illinois and forget Craggmoor. I'd learned long ago to listen to Aunt Coral. She knew—somehow—that Craggmoor was no good. Some obedient niece I turned out to be.

"Merri doesn't even have a car!" Garth went on. "Did you expect her to walk back to the Springs?"

Rosinna's fury crumbled. "I had no idea!"

Garth drew her aside to continue.

"I really should go," I cried, reaching for the door before he could begin.

Rosinna raised her eyebrows hopefully. Garth scowled.

"I'm just causing trouble," I said.

"No, you're not," Garth barked. "Sis and I always exchange friendly threats this way, don't we, dear?"

If he was Rosinna's brother…My heart sank. I tugged at

the door. The sooner I got out of there...

"You are only a stepbrother." Rosinna smiled up at Garth coldly. "Don't forget that. Since Stewart's illness you're hardly more than an employee as far as I'm concerned."

"What she means is, as the estate's attorney, I'm just hired help. I really am part of the family though." He grinned. "However remotely," he added to Rosinna. He yanked off his gloves and tossed them at Rosinna. "Merry and I are half related through our mother," he explained, looking at me with a sardonic smile. His gloves dropped to the floor. "No one approved of my mother, Natalie. Stewart took to drink after her death—and now there's just us children: Rosinna," he said, clicking his heels in a mock salute. "Jerome..." He rolled a grimace over his shoulder toward the staircase. "Merrisa, and me—plain old Garth."

I smothered a laugh. He was a tease.

"And now *you*," he added, pulling off his topcoat.

He wore a brown sport jacket over a tight gray turtleneck. It fit him perfectly. I found myself liking everything about him—even his acid tongue.

"Please, Rosinna," Garth went on loudly. "Let the young lady stay the night. It really is dangerous out there. We wouldn't want to lose two Merrys."

"Very well." She sighed in defeat. "If Miss Glenden wishes to stay..."

I knew she wanted me to refuse. I was about to grant her wish when something in the back of my mind told me to stick it out just a bit longer.

"Could I stay long enough to meet Mr. Glenden? That's one mess I'd really like to clear up."

Garth made an elaborate nod, as if he approved of my

skillful maneuver.

Rosinna nodded out of politeness. Above all, she valued proper behavior. Maybe that's why I instinctively distrusted her. I felt more comfortable with an open, honest person like Garth. I just hoped I'd never come under the lash of his tongue.

"I'll see if Stewart is up to visitors," Rosinna said. "Forgive me, Merri, for not offering earlier. It slipped my mind. He's eager to meet you. Maybe it *will* do him some good. Ever since I explained that your call was not from Merry herself, he's been incredibly depressed. Seeing you will help him over the disappointment."

How did she know so certainly that Merry hadn't called?

Garth looked around and frowned after she went up the stairs. "Rosinna has the heat off again. For a lady of wealth and leisure she sure is chintzy. Frugal, she would say. She got that trait from her mother. It's for sure no Glenden ever taught her that. Glendens are notoriously generous—as you can see by this cavernous house. Let's go back to the den. I'll have Florence make us coffee."

Coffee—tea; I was going in circles. Obediently I followed him, eager for the warmth of the fire and Garth's more polite conversation.

"Tell me what you do," Garth said when we settled in the room where I'd had tea with Rosinna earlier. He stoked the fire and then rubbed broad hands together before it.

I filled in what information I had left out when we talked outside. As I talked, I relaxed and again found myself looking him over and finding everything about him picture perfect.

"I've only done a few oils," I said, describing my past efforts at painting. "Usually afterward I'll see other works that put mine to shame and then I give it up for a while. Commercial art is a field where I think I could do well." I had begun to lean forward in my chair and Garth was listening with genuine interest. "I could..."

"This is all very cozy," Rosinna commented, as she came in, looking the two of us over contemptuously.

Garth propped his elbow against the mantelpiece. "I thought perhaps I'd better warm the place up a bit." He smiled at me devilishly. "You wouldn't want Merri to think we aren't well enough off to keep our humble home warm."

She reddened.

"Where's old Jerry while we bask in this glowing comfort?" Garth asked.

Rosinna eased him aside and adjusted the fire screen. She swept off the hearth where he had dropped splinters and disturbed ashes putting logs on the fire. "He is in his room working. He'll be down for dinner."

"Have you met Jerry?" Garth asked me.

I shook my head. I shifted uneasily, stared at the carpet, and then picked at the sleeve of my coat. Garth and Rosinna started in on each other again—over the heat this time. My back began to ache.

"You're a terrible host," Rosinna scolded in a crescendo of insults. She crossed the room and reached for my coat. "You let her sit here with her things and offer her nothing to drink. What she must think of us!"

"Coffee's on the way." Garth sighed. He tossed a soft, apologetic look across the room to me. I felt warmer.

"Probably none was made," Rosinna snipped.

"You and your tea," he snorted. "You should be living somewhere back in jolly old England, not here in the wild west."

Rosinna sighed and made a private face to me. "While Garth's coffee is brewing, let's go up and see Stewart. He's ready to see you now," Rosinna said, carrying my coat out into the hall where she hung it in a wide fur-filled cedar closet under the staircase.

"Aren't I invited along?" Garth pouted.

"Oh, really," she snapped impatiently. "You may do anything in this house that you please."

"No kidding?" He grinned.

She paused, her expression growing haughty. "It's as much your house as mine."

"Then I propose we turn on the heat."

"Now, Garth," she said, continuing into the main hall and turning toward the staircase, gracefully, as if she'd had lessons on how to pause at the foot of stairs.

"I'm cold, and I'm sure Merri is, too. She's not dressed for the winter climate inside this mausoleum. It's colder than—"

"Very well! But it is useless, heating forty-seven rooms for four people."

"Don't forget our devoted Florence and Jean," Garth reminded her. "I hear servants feel the cold as much as we. Surely, you can figure out some way to heat just the front rooms. I don't expect you to open the ballroom—not tonight, anyway," he added, winking at me.

"A ballroom!" I exclaimed. "Pool and tennis courts? Stables?"

Rosinna smiled proudly. "This is truly a mansion in the old style. I'll show you around later, if you'd like."

I nodded eagerly. "If it wouldn't be too much trouble." That pleased her.

"Stewart's waiting," she said, turning.

"If he can't have Baby Sister, perhaps cousin Merri from Illinois will raise his spirits," Garth said, smirking just enough to anger Rosinna again.

"Has he been sick long?" I asked, turning to Garth as his hand touched my elbow. We started up and I couldn't help smile.

"I'm afraid so," Rosinna answered for Garth when we reached the top of the stairs.

She led us down a paneled hall carpeted with a blue and cream Oriental runner. Brocade chairs and fine old paintings so obviously Victorian that even I recognized the style lined the walls.

"He nearly died two years ago. He never would have recovered if Merry hadn't stayed with him night and day. She was devoted to him. After she left he had a relapse and hardly has the will left now to go on. He's only living for the day he sees her again."

"I'm not going to make him worse, am I?" I asked.

"I'm sure you won't. Seeing you may restore some of his enthusiasm. Maybe he'll even come down for dinner. I've instructed Florence to fix a family favorite. Yes, I'm sure he'll be happy to see you. *I* certainly haven't been able to take Merry's place."

"All this chit-chat is really nice, Rosinna," Garth suddenly hissed, pulling her back from the door. "But why don't you just *tell* her?"

Rosinna pleaded with her eyes.

"Stewart is an alcoholic," Garth whispered.

"Oh, please," Rosinna moaned, turning away.

It seemed as though no matter how hard she tried she

couldn't keep things polite and pleasant. At every turn Garth exposed her pretenses with malicious glee.

I didn't see anything so terrible in letting her keep up appearances, if it meant that much to her. Yet I didn't see anything so shameful in admitting Stewart had a drinking problem. I figured it was probably a good thing I knew.

"She's going to know as soon as you open that door," Garth said, still gripping Rosinna's arm. "If you didn't stand on decorum and fancy manners all the time maybe you'd be more...useful."

Rosinna's eyes were like knives as she raised them to Garth. With amazing self-control, she shook herself free and turned once again to the door. Opening it, she called softly, "Stewart? We're all here."

I trembled a little as Garth's hand touched the small of my back and relentlessly guided me into the dim room.

"This is cousin Merri, Father," Rosinna said, going inside.

A tall, thin man turned from the wide front windows and faced me. He didn't look drunk. His slightly gray dark hair, lean tormented face, and small sad eyes made him appealingly handsome. He walked across the room as if it were a very great distance he had been traveling a long time.

"Merri? You really surprised me when you called," he said in that gentle, weakened voice I remembered. He held out his hands and I took them. He hugged me gently, leaving me surprised and touched. I purposely ignored the odor of alcohol about him.

"This has been the craziest day!" I laughed. "I've got everyone so confused."

"Me most of all." Stewart smiled. "Hello, Garth. What brings you up today?"

"Merri." Garth nodded toward me with a strange, almost protective look on his face. My heart skipped a beat and began to race. "When she made her reservations the detective and I knew someone was on the way. I wasn't able to meet her at the airport. I do have other clients..." He chuckled, noticing Rosinna squirm at his tactless remark. "Anyway, I wanted to see her for myself."

"You knew who I was all along!" I cried.

Garth grinned. "Not exactly. Only your name."

Stewart smiled and touched my arm. "Garth is a crafty young man. That's why I let him handle all my business." He swayed a little and blinked slowly.

"If you'll excuse me, Father, I need to speak to Garth." Rosinna's head was cocked stiffly. "You and Merri chat a little." She stepped quickly from the room almost as if she were holding her breath.

With a small shrug, Garth followed her. "We've talked Merri into staying the night, Stewart. Will you join us for dinner?"

Stewart considered that. "I think I will. Now, young lady, tell me who you are. Are you really a Glenden?"

Again I repeated my story. "I came to see if I could find Merry," I added at the end. "But it looks like I won't."

Stewart poured himself a drink. He motioned me to a plush recliner and then sank to the edge of his bed. He hardly made a dent in it. He was no more than a wisp, a shadow of a smile. Only the glow of intoxication gave his eyes a sign of life.

His room was decorated in deeply masculine brown and creams. Here and there a touch of orange brightened the shadows. He kept the lights low. A stereo across the room played softly.

As my eyes turned back to him, I felt a deep sense of helplessness. I finally had to stop watching him swirl the slippery gold with a hand that shook as if it were cold.

"Rosinna told me about Merry," I said softly. "I wish I could help."

"You may not realize it," Stewart said, looking up at me, "but you *are* helping."

"Rosinna doesn't think so. She'll be glad when I'm gone."

"Ignore her," he said.

"And Garth! One minute he's nice—then he turns right around and cuts Rosinna to the bone!"

Stewart chuckled. "Rosinna and Garth. Don't let them bother you. It's aggravating to hear them bicker, I know. In recent years they've refined their fights almost to an art form, but they're harmless. They've been at each other's throats since I can remember. She's excessively proper, and Garth is"—he shook his head—"himself."

"He's your attorney?"

"Oh, you knew that? Yes. Smart guy. I don't know what I'd do without him. Rosinna and Jerome are the children of my first wife. Not a brain in their heads for business. Germaine…" He struggled for words. "She was like Rosinna."

I nodded.

"Or should I say Rosinna is like her mother?" He chuckled without amusement, sagging a little.

"I know what you mean."

"Of course you do. Rosinna complains that I never say precisely what I mean, but I do. She just doesn't want to hear what I say."

I straightened the hem of my skirt and studied my spotted shoes awkwardly.

"Garth and Rosinna go at each other just like Germaine and I used to...before she died. That's Rosinna's trouble. She didn't have her mother long enough. When I married Natalie it was too late. They didn't get along. There we were, me and Natalie, oblivious to anyone else. Rosinna and Jerry were like little robots, yes, sir, no, sir, would you care for tea, sir. Those kids!"

I could almost picture those squabbling kids as they grew into squabbling adults—the cultured and the uncultured forever clashing.

"Natalie wasn't like the rest of us." Stewart sighed. "She was young and pretty—so pretty. She didn't have money. She was a widow at twenty-five. Garth was five or six when I met her, as different from Rosie and Jerry as a kid could get. I've always liked him—almost more my son than Jerome."

"I'm glad it's not my fault they're arguing."

"No, it's not you. They just plain hate each other. That's why I put my baby Merry in charge of the money. She could always tease them into some kind of truce. I knew she'd keep things running smoothly after I was gone."

"You're a young man!" I exclaimed. "You've got years and years left."

He stared up at me in surprise. Then he smiled so broadly the glazed look left his eyes. "You're a good girl. Just like my Merry. Won't you stay longer than just tonight?"

I didn't know how to refuse him.

"I know, I know," he said, waving a tired hand. "Who wants to listen to an old man's sad stories?"

"That's not it, Mr. Glenden, really. I'd love to stay. I mean,

I didn't come here intending to...barge in or anything."

"I know what you mean." He smiled, winking, as if we already shared a secret.

"You know, when you told me Merry was gone, I was angry. I just lost my aunt recently and I loved her more than anything. I never would have left her. I couldn't understand how Merry could leave you."

He raised his glass and looked at its contents thoughtfully. "Perhaps it won't take long—to understand."

"I'll stay if you think we can convince Rosinna I'm okay."

"Never mind Rosinna!" Stewart barked. "I am her father and I can handle her, if I have to. She takes everything so seriously. We don't get out any more because she's so afraid of publicity—afraid of gawkers, as she calls them."

I agreed with him there.

"You know what's wrong with her? She takes herself too seriously. She doesn't have any friends—no men in her life. The only person she talks to is that idiot Jerome. Ah, I don't know how that boy can be my son. Have you met him?"

"No."

"My son!" He sniffed.

Jerome sounded like a real winner.

"You and my baby don't look much alike, but you're the same inside. I like that. Tell Rosinna I want you to stay—for as long as you like. Better yet, I'll tell her myself."

"I'd love to see the grounds. I brought a sketch pad. Maybe I could draw something for you."

Suddenly he placed a shaking hand over his eyes. "Merry."

"We can find her," I reassured him.

He shook his head slowly and took a deep breath. "She's gone. She didn't defy us and run away. It was too sudden.

I'd just been home from the hospital a few weeks. She was always with me, determined I get well and never take another drink."

"Then, what happened?"

"She just disappeared. The police said she took clothes, a suitcase. I didn't believe it. How could she? I needed her. I needed her!"

I shook his arm. "Please, don't."

"I can't help it. My baby's gone. She's never coming back."

"I may not be very smart," I said, "but I'm going to find Merry."

"It's no use," he moaned.

"You can't ever give up. Let's go downstairs and talk to Garth."

He straightened and smiled sadly. "I'm glad you're here. I think too much and talk too much. There's nobody here to listen. I could drive myself crazy that way."

"Hey, you two!" Garth laughed, coming back into the room abruptly. "Rosinna says dinner will be ready soon. I hear the hermit is coming down from his studio. Stewart, how do you like our new Merri?"

"I'd say she's every bit as nice as her cousin. They'd make a pair, wouldn't they?"

Garth grinned. "Contrasting, but very pretty."

"What does Merry look like?" I asked.

Garth made a sudden cautionary sign behind Stewart. "Later," he mouthed.

"I...ah, don't keep a picture handy," Stewart said, not noticing Garth's signals.

"I can show her later," Garth said, offering Stewart his arm. "Let's go before Rosinna declares a household emergency."

I followed the two of them out.

"How are you feeling?" Garth asked as he steadied his stepfather. "You're looking good." He smiled at Stewart with genuine concern.

I let them get ahead of me when I noticed a particularly beautiful painting hanging near the staircase. When I saw the Glenden name scrawled in the corner I was thrilled. It was a wonderful sensation to belong to something that went as far back as this big house and proud family. I never before realized how I'd missed having a heritage.

"Hurry up, Merri," Garth called. "I don't want you to get lost."

Stewart had already gone down. Garth waited for me to catch up. When I joined him he slid his arm around me. "Can you imagine the grand wedding processions that have gone down this staircase?" he asked unexpectedly.

"Have there been many?"

"Oh, let's see. The first was Clinton's wedding-back in the late 1800s. He met his bride, Merrisa Stevens, in either New York or New Orleans, I've forgotten. They were married here right after the place was built. Then George, Clinton's younger son, and his bride Allison were married here. George was a stern old character. I've read his journals so I know his innermost thoughts—mercenary to the core. It must not have bothered him a bit to have his brother break with the family."

"You mean my grandfather."

"If it weren't for his mother's diary I never would have known about David."

"You don't think I'm an impostor?"

"Rosinna insisted I check you out." His eyes flashed.

"She's scandalized that I've let you stay. Now, promise me you won't steal the family silver before your papers are cleared."

"Verified," I corrected.

"Yes, that's her word."

"But I really am…"

"No question in my mind, Merri dear. But to please Rosinna I will do what she wishes, verify you, just to throw it in her face. Rosinna gives me little credit for brains. I graduated from Harvard Law, yet I'm an incompetent in her eyes."

"A Harvard man." I smiled saucily.

"Are you impressed?" he asked, eyeing me with a twinkle. "Then it was worth it. Yes, Harvard. Before that, the finest military academies…"

"You?"

"Why so surprised?"

"You're too…"

"Too what?" He smiled.

The staircase became eternally long and I blushed all the way to the bottom. "You don't look military."

"Did I say it did me any good?" He chuckled. "You must learn to listen, Miss Merri Glenden of Illinois. I said academies, plural. I have records at most of them. I'm remembered from California to Maine—Garth Favor: incorrigible. Nevertheless, Stewart liked me. Rosinna could hardly hold up her head while I attended public high school. Valedictorian did nothing to improve her opinion of me either."

"Now I *am* impressed."

"Good! At least somebody appreciates me."

We were just crossing the entrance hall when the

skinniest man I had ever seen came from the brilliantly lit dining hall. "So it's you." He sniffed, looking down his hawkish nose at Garth.

"Me, what?"

"You and your boasting and crass behavior echoing throughout this house."

Garth burst into a grin. "Your history isn't nearly as colorful."

"Indeed."

"So, Merri. Meet your remaining cousin, Jerome Glenden: artist, writer, thinker and..." He smiled and seemed to be holding himself back.

Jerome crossed the hall as silently as if floating. For a moment I wondered if he was real. He wore a maroon sweater over a white shirt that sported heavy silver cufflinks. His trousers were a deep pink and too short. They looked new, yet several years out of style. He smelled of shoe polish and sickly sweet after-shave.

I couldn't help feeling fascinated by his neck, which was so long he looked like a jack-in-the-box. His sandy blond hair fell loosely over his forehead. He was all teeth and nose and not enough eyes, like a badly done caricature.

"How nice to meet you," Jerome said. "Garth, what did you say your young lady's name was?"

"She isn't mine, Jerry, old pal. She is Merri—Merrisa Glenden of Illinois, granddaughter of old David, who scorned all this so long ago."

Jerome regarded me, his eyebrows just like Rosinna's, quizzical. They were a pair, I thought. He and his sister were probably best of friends, impeccable to the last hair, exact in their manners, effective in their ability to make me feel out of place and unwanted.

"The author of those peculiar letters," he said finally.

"Very good, Jerry! You're quick today. Written any great novels lately?"

"I'm having a bad time of it these past weeks," he complained in a way that didn't spark my sympathy.

Garth gave me a look and I almost had to laugh. "Did your pencil break?" Garth asked with mock concern.

Jerome's nostrils flared. "I'm sure we're quite late for dinner. We're dining formally tonight." He glanced over me once more, briefly, and then sighed at Garth. "Keep a civil tongue about you, stepbrother. Rosinna has given great care to entertain this young lady properly. Don't spoil it."

"By all means, let's do be proper," Garth said dryly. He offered me his arm, his wrists arched and pinkie raised. We followed Jerome into the dining room, nearly bubbling over with laughter. Just before Garth seated me I drew him back.

"What is it?"

I cringed at his sudden abrupt tone. "How much has really been done to find cousin Merry?" I said timidly, my amusement gone.

He smiled, relaxing his tight expression. "I thought you were going to scold me for being such a pain. Jerry rubs me the wrong way almost more than Rosinna does."

"I wouldn't..."

"No, of course not. You're too nice for that."

"I don't know about that. The reason I ask is, Stewart needs her, badly."

"You're right about that."

"He wants me to stay. And really, I haven't anything else to do..."

"I thought you were in school."

"I was, but when Aunt Coral died I stopped going."

"I'm sorry."

I shrugged. "I'd be glad to stay…except…"

"You can't stand Rosinna."

"Not that. She's not so bad at times."

"I hadn't noticed," he grumbled.

"But she does think I'm butting my nose in where it doesn't belong. She probably thinks I've got an ulterior motive."

"Do you?"

I made an impatient face.

"I like that feisty look in your eyes." He grinned. "Is there someone waiting for you back in little town, Illinois? A male someone?"

"No," I said softly. "Like I said, I can stay. I don't know how well I'll fit in here though. You see before you Merri Glenden in her best dress—which isn't much."

"Don't let them bother you about that."

"Well…" I tossed my head. "This *is* sort of an elegant place, and all of you wear your clothes like you don't even notice how nice they are."

"How would you wear good clothes?"

"Never mind. Do you think there's any way we could do more than the detective, in finding Merry? It may make Stewart feel better for a while if I'm around, but I won't do forever."

"And you shouldn't have to. The only real evidence we had was the missing suitcase. Rosinna can tell you more about that. Merry disappeared in late January, two years ago. The area was combed. We had more servants then and everyone was questioned. I don't know why, but afterward Rosinna fired everyone, even our full-time gardener—except for her maid and cook, naturally."

"A gardener even in winter?"

"Colorado snows are notoriously sudden and heavy. A blizzard like the one right now will ruin hundreds of trees. He was handy for keeping the lake clean and plowing the drive too. Anyway, the detective didn't turn up anything at the airports or bus depots. Merry vanished without a trace."

I shivered. "It's creepy."

"And sad. I liked her. She was a good kid."

"Do you think I could look around later?"

"Ask Rosinna for a tour. She's got the heat on in this section at least. I'd take you around myself, but I have to work tomorrow. The roads may be bad, so I'll have to leave right after dinner."

"Don't you live here?"

"Are you kidding? Have a maid pick up my socks and serve me tea in bed? I like Craggmoor. It's a nice place to visit, but I hated living here. An illustrious stepbrother and spiteful stepsister are too much. I've got an apartment in the Springs. Rosinna loathes it."

I laughed. "You love to tease her."

"Tease? My dear, I mean every word. I'm very aware of what kind of person my stepsister is. Jerry is her carbon copy. They bore and irritate me. I'm much happier when I'm not here. The only reason I show up at all is for Stewart's sake. Ordinarily, I'd avoid a dinner here like a plague, but you make me hunger for Florence's cuisine and the company of my intolerable relatives."

When Rosinna came in our conversation ended. She

seated me next to Garth across from herself and Jerome. Stewart headed the table and said an awkward grace: "Thank you, Lord, for the renewed hope."

My chest felt suddenly tight.

After a thoughtful silence, Rosinna turned her gray eyes to me. "Tell me, Merri. What kind of art were you studying in Chicago? Some very fine schools there, I've heard."

I tore my eyes from Stewart's craggy face and began to tell them all about my life in North Lake. Once Rosinna heard I was studying commercial art, she stopped listening. Jerome just ate. Occasionally he stared at me with the dullest, most watered-down blue eyes I had ever seen. His dopey expression made me think that if I hadn't heard him speak I would have sworn he didn't have a brain in his head. I had to watch myself that I didn't become too fascinated by the way his Adam's apple wiggled every time he swallowed. I felt ashamed, amusing myself at his expense. Partly I blamed that on Garth, but Jerome was definitely a "character" type, someone an artist would draw to study what was not normal or beautiful.

Garth hardly talked at all during dinner. He looked at me now and then and I'd lose track of the conversation. He was making the supreme effort to be civil. Sometimes I'd catch his wry smile or an amused twinkle in his eyes. I could almost hear his silent remarks; it was as if we didn't even need to talk.

Rosinna and Jerome behaved pretentiously during dinner, using long dictionary words, dropping famous names, and affecting elegant manners. I kept reminding myself that I didn't have the education or background they had, but it didn't make them easier to tolerate.

"You're too quiet," Stewart said, as the maid cleared the feast away and served coffee afterward.

"I think I'm getting tired." I smiled weakly.

"Forgive me, Merri!" Rosinna cried. "I should have shown you to your room long before now. You must be worn out. I'm a terrible hostess. It's just that we've had so few guests since...And we're all fascinated with your story."

"Did I tell you I want Merri to stay?" Stewart interrupted.

Rosinna's face tightened.

"Would you like to?" Stewart asked, raising his eyebrows. He tried to hold a flame to his bent cigarette.

"Father, please. Not at the table." Rosinna sighed, swishing her hand through the air.

"Rosinna!" Stewart groaned. "Relax. But be a lady for a moment more and invite your long-lost cousin to stay the night—a week, if she'll have us."

"Of course, Father. Merri, we'd be happy for you to stay."

"You really wouldn't mind?"

"You're welcome here as long as you like. We're at your disposal."

"Then just for a little while," I said, a smile tugging at my lips as I ventured a peek at Garth.

Jerome got up noiselessly. "I have work to do."

My smile faded under his resentful gaze.

"You must show Merri your studio tomorrow," Rosinna said. "He is quite an artist, Merri."

"It must run in the family."

"Unfortunately, I'm hopelessly inept." Rosinna sighed.

"Did you do the one up in the hall, Jerome?" I asked.

He straightened indignantly—looking like an annoyed

rooster. "No, my great-grandmother did that. Her talent is unmatched, even by me."

"Good night, Jerry!" Garth called loudly.

"Are you going back to the city tonight?" Jerome asked, lowering his small eyes to Garth as if it took great effort to look at someone so far beneath him.

"Yes, aren't you glad?"

"Really, Garth," Rosinna said.

"Leave him alone." Stewart sighed. "Excuse me too, Merri. Fine dinner, Rosinna. Let's do it more often."

"Of course, Father. As often as you wish."

"There, you see?" Stewart winked. "It's my fault we don't eat together."

At that I expected to see amusement on Garth's face. Instead his lips tightened and he scowled. I didn't like the deep line that formed beside his mouth. Again I was convinced I'd never like being on the wrong side of him.

Stewart left, nodding slightly. "I'll see you tomorrow, Merri."

When the three of us were alone, the scene erupted. "Have you been keeping Stewart in his room again?" Garth demanded.

Rosinna's eyes darted uneasily. "Really! Must you?"

"If I don't come up here every day you shut him away!"

"Please, not in front of—"

"Why shouldn't Merri hear what really goes on here? She's one of us now. She came here because of Merry and Stewart—which is more than you'd do if you were in her place."

"You have no right!"

"I have every right! Stewart deserves better. He's gone

through more torture than you'll ever dream up. Losing Natalie was bad enough, but after Merry—it's a wonder he's still walking around!"

"He only eats in his room when—"

"He's drunk? And why's that? So you don't have to look at him…or smell him, or be reminded that he isn't the grand master of Craggmoor?"

"Oh, Garth. You're uncouth."

He barked an unpleasant laugh. "I'm a full-fledged honest-to-God monster. You and I know it."

"I won't listen to this," she hissed, trying to slide past him. He held her arm for a moment.

"Could you show me my room now?" I interrupted. "I'm awfully sleepy."

"Of course." Rosinna motioned me toward the staircase. "You're room is this way. If you'll let me pass, Garth…"

He released her. As she walked up the stairs, her back was ramrod straight, her arms stiff at her sides, fists clenched. Red finger marks showed on her wrist.

She opened a door across the hall from Stewart's room. "I have the forward rooms heated now," she said, spitting out each work deliberately. "Your bath is through that door. I took the liberty of having your things brought up. Please feel free to use anything you wish. If you're hungry later, just ring. If you'll excuse me now, I'm going to bed." She nodded coldly.

Her eyes were red. Garth had actually made her cry! I felt sorry for her—a little. She tried hard.

"Rosinna," I said hastily, and then fumbled for words. "If you'd feel better, I'll go home tomorrow."

"Don't concern yourself, Merri. As Garth said, you've

done for Stewart what I've been unable to do for two years. He's smiling again. You mustn't worry about my feelings in the matter. What you witnessed between Garth and myself was our usual fare."

"But I do worry about your feelings."

She took a deep breath. "You're very kind. Good night, Merri. We have a little breakfast around eight, but feel free to sleep as late as you like. Tomorrow I'll give you the grand tour. Sleep well."

"Good night, Rosinna."

She walked stiffly to the end of the hall and disappeared around the corner toward what I assumed were the back recesses of Craggmoor. Moments later a door closed softly.

Suddenly Garth came bounding up the stairs. "Merri, I just wanted to say good night. I'll be back tomorrow. Take care. And Merri? I'm sorry about the argument. I guess I let it get out of hand."

I mumbled something and then watched him hurry downstairs. The softest whisper of cold air swirled up from the opened front door when he went out.

With a ragged sigh I went in and closed my door. My room looked like something out of a decorator's magazine. I tiptoed across the white carpet afraid I would mess it up. A wide sweep of windows displayed the mountain behind Craggmoor. The room seemed as large as Aunt Coral's whole cottage! It had not only a king-size bed, but a love seat, table, and white brocade chair. The plush carpet looked like snow and felt as thick. It was in the bathroom too, where everything was either glass, blue tile, or chrome.

The window overlooked a stone balcony. Craggmoor wasn't just a huge block as I had thought seeing it from the front. It was U-shaped. Below in the center of the U was a snow-covered courtyard. The world outside was a swirl of white. I had never seen such a snowstorm. I felt swathed in a world alien from what I had known before. When it came time for me to change for bed I felt awkward and uneasy, as if someone were watching me. At last I locked myself in the bathroom with the few pitifully ordinary things I'd brought from home. I tried to touch as little as possible, noticing that everything I did touch glared back with smudges and fingerprints.

I had just come out when I heard the heavy knocker downstairs. I pressed my ear to my door. Snoop, I scolded myself.

Rosinna's footsteps, rustling beneath something silky (and probably expensive and beautiful) hurried down the hall. "Who is it, Jean?" she whispered.

"It's just me," Garth called, trudging up the stairs.

"You're getting snow all over the carpet!"

"Then have it replaced. I couldn't get my car out of the lot. It's snowed another foot since I arrived."

"You may use one of our cars."

"No, thanks. I'll just stick around."

"I'll have Jean see to your room then," Rosinna said after a taut pause.

"Never mind. I can find the bed myself—and don't send her in tomorrow morning. I'm a big boy and I can hang up my own towels."

"Very well, Garth. But do be quiet. I'm sure Merri's already asleep."

"Good night, Sis." Garth chuckled nearby. Then he slammed his door. I heard Rosinna sniff and sigh as she went back to her room.

As tired as I was I hated to commit myself to the strange bed. But once I slipped between cool crisp sheets, I felt like a queen. I felt sleep coming quickly and only had a second or two to think of Garth, the first really interesting man I had ever met. I wondered if he was thinking of me, too.

In the days ahead, however, I would question my impression of Garth Favor, Craggmoor's attorney.

Three

Something woke me in the night.

I had slept soundly, maybe because of the comfortable bed—or maybe it was because for the first time since Aunt Coral had died I had not fallen asleep wondering about the fire in the trunk. Becoming involved with my cousin's family was good therapy—or so I thought.

I threw off the blankets and sat on the edge of the bed. The room was cold! There was a special smell to the coldness. It wasn't like a house that had lost heat in the night. The smell had a fresh bite to it that reminded me of snow. I looked toward the door that led to the small balcony off my room. It was open! Bits of snow drifted to the carpet.

My heart hammered. This is ridiculous, I told myself. The balcony door must have blown open, but I felt suddenly uneasy. I walked around the bed to close the door and stepped right in a cold, damp spot on the carpet. Stooping, I ran my fingers over the wet place. Bits of snow melted on my fingertips.

I switched on the bedside lamp. The light dismissed the sinister shadows and my fears. Everything was exactly as I had left it. I had just about convinced myself that I had imagined the snow beside my bed when I *saw* snowy footprints marking a path across my room and going out into the hall. Someone had just come into my room from the balcony! I put on my robe, knowing I must tell Rosinna right away.

I left my light on and stepped into the dark hall. Once around the corner, I realized I had no idea which room was Rosinna's. I counted seven doors, paused at the first and second and heard nothing. One was probably Jerome's; I certainly didn't want to barge in on him.

Something about the last door made me stop. I touched the door and it swung open. The room was so dark I couldn't see a thing. Taking several steps inside, I was about to whisper Rosinna's name when massive arms went around me. A hand too strong for me to overcome clamped over my mouth. I couldn't make a sound and my struggles were useless.

"Don't scream," he hissed. He jerked me deeper into the darkness and seemed to enjoy hurting me. "Where is she?"

I shook my head.

"Don't lie any more. Where is Merry?"

I struggled and his grip tightened. I whimpered and felt my body gel with fear. Don't faint, I told myself.

"You thought I'd given up, didn't you? You thought you'd fooled me. I know you, Rosinna. You know where Merry is and I'm going to make you tell me."

I shook my head harder.

"If you've hurt her," he hissed, "I'll do the same to you."

How could he mistake me for Rosinna? She had dark

hair. Mine was blonde. Maybe the person holding me wasn't a man at all. Maybe Rosinna herself was trying to scare me away!

For a second he let go of me. Then as abruptly he took a handful of my hair. "You're not Rosinna! Who are you?"

We struggled across the room. My legs bumped against what felt like a bed. He pushed me face down into it. Harder and harder he pressed until I couldn't get a good breath.

"You'll be sorry. When I find her, you'll be sorry!"

Suddenly he was gone. I heard nothing more. I rolled over, gasping, cold with sweat, shaking with tears. I plunged from the shrouded room and stumbled down the hall toward the light. As I rounded the corner I ran right into Garth. I nearly screamed.

"What are you doing?" He forced me to stop.

I must have looked half crazy. I pushed him away and fell against the door of my room.

"You're trembling. What's wrong?"

It couldn't have been he, I told myself. It just couldn't!

Garth helped me into my room, where the light melted my fears. When he sat me down on the bed and looked into my eyes, I tried desperately to believe he hadn't attacked me.

"Tell me what happened," he insisted. "Where have you been?"

"I woke up," I panted softly. "My balcony door was open. Snow was blowing in. There, see? Snowy footprints on the carpet! I went to tell Rosinna. I was down the hall—in some room and someone grabbed me!"

His eyes widened. "Who grabbed you? Jerry?"

"I don't know!"

Something in my eyes must have betrayed that moment

when I suspected him. "Was it a man, you're sure?" he asked.

"He was strong...I was afraid! I think it could have been..."

When I paused, he put his hands on my shoulders and I felt very small and helpless. Without warning, he kissed me lightly. "It wasn't me," he said.

"I didn't think that!" I cried, shaking my head, but I stiffened slightly as he began to pull me closer to him.

"And *what* is going on in here?" came Rosinna's harsh voice from my doorway. "Garth, I am shocked!"

"Merri's had a scare," he said, jerking around. He tightened the belt of his robe and glared at Rosinna.

"Indeed?"

"Someone came in my room!" I gasped. "I was just coming to tell you when I got grabbed. I don't know what kind of people you've got hiding around here, but he was rough! I mean, I'm sorry if I went in where I didn't belong, but he threatened me! He..."

"See the marks on her face?" Garth said, grabbing my chin and turning my face for Rosinna to see the evidence.

I hadn't told him about the hand over my mouth, I thought. Were there really visible marks? Or were the two of them...Were Rosinna and Garth trying to frighten me for some reason?

"What I see," Rosinna snapped, "is some rather questionable behavior."

"How stupid you are." Garth sighed. He released my face and then slipped his arm around my shoulders almost like a protective brother. "Feeling okay now?"

"For once I have you, Garth." She smiled triumphantly. "Get out of this room before Stewart wakes up."

"I think you'd better get down from your pious pile of

manners and look at this girl!" Garth said. "She's had a bad scare and you worry about…Rosinna, you've got granite for brains and you're about as sensitive as a cactus. Would Merri make up such a story?"

"Very well, *who* came into your room, Merri?" she asked, turning her haughty uplifted eyebrows to me.

"A prowler, I think. He came in from the balcony."

"Nonsense! That door is always locked. The balcony is twenty feet above ground and besides, no one could get in without setting off the alarm. You've simply had a nightmare…one precipitated by my stepbrother's intrusion."

She marched across the room and jerked at the door, which was securely locked. She fumbled with the latch and then wrenched it open. "I see nothing here."

"There are some spots on the carpet," I said. "Snow doesn't get all the way over here all by itself."

She checked over the spots—with her eyes closed, I figured.

Exasperated, Garth snorted. "If you're through with your idiotic investigation…"

"I'm sorry, Merri. I really don't see any proof…" Rosinna stifled a yawn.

I could feel rude, angry words bubbling up. I looked away from Rosinna before I said anything more. "Never mind then."

From the corner of my eye, I saw her smile. "Are you coming, Garth?" she said crisply.

"I'll have the police here in twenty minutes," Garth said with his hand on my shoulder. "Unless you think it was Jerry, in which case, I'll cheerfully go wring his neck."

"Really," Rosinna exclaimed. "You think *my*

brother would…"

"Forget it," I said stiffly. "I know you don't believe me. So what's the use?"

"*I* believe you!" Garth said.

I waved him off. "I'm all right. I don't want any more trouble. Go back to bed."

"Call if you need me," Garth said, following Rosinna with a shrug. "I'm in the next room."

"I know," I said, avoiding his eyes.

They both left me, Rosinna looking superior, but Garth puzzled and suspicious.

I locked the door after them, then I peeked through the keyhole to see if there was a key in the other side. There wasn't, just a tiny view of a walnut chair across the dim hall.

I checked the balcony door again. I yanked at it and could see that it was so solid it never would have "blown" open. For several minutes I looked out the window. It had stopped snowing. The cap of snow on the edge of the balcony wall was perfect and undisturbed. No one could have climbed over that without brushing some of the snow off.

The snow on the floor of the balcony, however, was lumpy. Could footprints be hidden under that last layer of white?

I pulled the drapes closed and paced for a while. I dreaded getting back in bed. What might happen while I was asleep this time?

Thirsty, I went into the bathroom for some water. It was so icy it hurt as I drank. When I looked in the mirror, I saw the fingermarks across my cheek. My stomach knotted. My arm stung, as I remembered the bruising strength of that hand. I had marks on my arm, and I pressed them to convince myself that were real. They were marks just like those Garth had left on Rosinna's arm after dinner.

Either he was the slickest liar I had ever met, or there were two men at Craggmoor capable of bruising an arm like that.

I left the light on in the bathroom when I got back into bed. I lay stiffly, staring at the ceiling, waiting for dawn and wondering how fast I could get out of that place.

Before I knew it, my room was bright with morning. I had slept after all! I felt a little better. The events of the night seemed less serious as I got up and stared out of my window again. The sun reflected off the snowy mountainside behind Craggmoor. I had to squint against the glare. The trees were dense black-green shapes looming over Craggmoor's humorless stones.

A prowler had come into my room the night before, I reminded myself. A "prowler." Why didn't Rosinna want to admit such a thing? Was it a blemish on the perfection of her mansion? Weren't such things *allowed* to happen?

I turned abruptly from the view and went back to the bed. It was still early. I didn't feel like going down. I sat and drew my knees up and stared at my locked door. I couldn't remember a time when Aunt Coral or I had ever had to lock our doors to each other. Except for the trunk, and that was another matter, I'd never before needed barriers between myself and others. In everything Aunt Coral and I had always been open and honest with each other.

If someone wanted to frighten me away from Craggmoor

they had done a good job. I had enough brains to keep my nose out of things and go home where I belonged. Aunt Coral had tried to prevent all this. If only I'd listened...

As I dressed I got that scruffy feeling again. I could almost picture Rosinna as she would look at breakfast—perfect down to the last buffed fingernail—while I...My hair looked limp and oily.

An assortment of shampoos lined the glass shelves in the bathroom. A hint? I needed a hair dryer if I was going to look presentable. I wondered if Rosinna had one. A quick look showed that the drawers in my room were empty. I felt like a snoop, and that was a sure sign that I wasn't comfortable at Craggmoor—and where I wasn't comfortable, I didn't want to be.

Wearing what had once been my favorite and most comfortable robe but was now just a ratty excuse for "suitable attire," I crept down the quiet hall, hoping I might find the maid. Once down the big staircase, I tiptoed toward the back. As I neared the closed kitchen door I heard angry voices. Despite all of Aunt Coral's years of teaching me good manners, I listened.

"Leave me in peace, Rosinna," Garth snarled from beyond the door. "I don't want to talk business, or anything else with you after last night. I'm tired from staring out my balcony door all night. You may not care what happens to the people in this house, but I do." There was a pause. "Let me have my coffee and I'll be out of your hair in ten minutes."

"I simply cannot handle this household any longer without knowledge of the accounts. You complain about the heat. Well, how can I do anything here when you have me believing we can't pay for it? I won't be in debt!"

"What possible difference would it make?" Garth demanded. "The bills are sent to my office. Wolves aren't at the door, yet. Leave me alone! Your questions give me a headache. You give me a first-class pain. You don't care how much it costs to heat this dump. You just didn't like getting caught with the heat off when unexpected company showed up. I know what you really want—your money. Correct? If you want to know about the accounts come by my office whenever you like. I'm open from nine to five. I'll be happy to set up an appointment with the accountant and he can tell you everything your mercenary little heart wishes to know."

"If you don't include me in the business dealings concerning the family money, I'll simply have to tell Stewart."

"Yes, do." Garth laughed. "I'm sure Stewart will be terribly concerned. You always were such a *help* with the investments. He'll treasure your opinions."

"He isn't the least bit aware of how you're keeping the facts from me," she snapped. "I only meant that he should be told, so that if an investigation is in order…"

"'I'm telling. I'm telling,'" Garth mimicked. "'I'll tell Daddy if you don't stop. You're a brat and I don't like you.'"

"When are you going to grow up, Garth?" Rosinna snapped.

"As soon as you do, I guess." He chuckled. "Half the time I don't see how you can call yourself a lady. Oh, you put on a good show with all your finishing-school grammar, but underneath you're just as petty and, sorry to say, human as the rest of us."

"You bore me."

"So do you. Why, then, don't you go up to your room and feel sorry for yourself for a while? Or you can go to dear brother and cry out all your enormous troubles. Better yet, tell Stewart I won't give you a dollar by dollar account of *his* money. You wouldn't understand anyway, even if I did."

"He has entrusted it to all of us, Garth. I have a right to know what you're doing with it."

"True, but I don't intend to tell you. So until it becomes yours—legally after Stewart dies—you'll just have to imagine the worst. Relax, dear. Remember, I only handle the money. I don't spend it as I wish. I assure you that if I did, you wouldn't be bothering me with your feeble questions. You'd have me in court."

"Obviously you're just being childish. We ought to be able to use some of it now. Why wait until Stewart is gone? He won't enjoy it then, will he?"

"Does he enjoy it now?"

"Certainly not, not if I'm afraid to—"

"That's your problem, not mine."

"He intended that we use it. That's why he turned it over to us."

"After Natalie died and he wound up in the hospital half dead from booze, he turned it over. The only reason he didn't revoke the agreement is because he knows he could still go any time. Pretty thought, yes? I know, Rosinna dear. It was I, you recall, who suggested we four control it equally. Terrible blunder. I should have let *you* have it all. You could have champagne for breakfast, a diamond-studded steering wheel on your Rolls Royce and the Vice President could come for tea."

"I would do no such thing," Rosinna pouted.

"In that case, you agree that Stewart was right when he put me in charge of the legal end. I shouldn't be badgered to death now. He trusted me and I'm trained to deal with the financial problems. But, of course, that doesn't matter to you, does it? The fact that he put Merry at the top of the heap has always galled you. You're without your precious millions. And Stewart, holding on by the thinnest of threads, is still with us. Perhaps you do not appreciate what an accomplishment that is, since you're just counting the days until—"

"How dare you?"

"But you're so good at counting. With Natalie..."

"Not that again."

"You didn't like her. She wasn't upper-class like you and your fancy Boston-bred mother. Natalie wasn't anything except beautiful and kind. That is a lot more than you'll ever be, even with your pedigree."

"I don't have to take such insults," she gasped. "I cared for Natalie. She was always very sweet to me. I love Stewart, too," Rosinna continued, her voice rising to a shriek. "It's just that—"

"You sound exactly the same as you did when you were twelve. Maybe you should engage an elocutionist, a mature one. If you'll excuse me, Sis, I'll be on my way. I'm tired of this useless argument. It's much less interesting than the ones we usually have. I do have to get back to my clients. Unlike some people around here, I work."

"At what, I wonder."

"I'll bite." He chuckled. "Tell me what you suspect."

"I think your investments are going poorly. You're ashamed to tell us you can't handle them any longer."

"Because I wasn't born to it?" Garth roared with amusement. "Oh, Rosinna. You continue to surprise me.

You're so shallow and take such small pains to conceal it. But, alas…" He sighed dramatically. "You've uncovered my shame."

"What is that?"

"The money, of course. It's all gone. I've squandered it."

"You're joking! I don't appreciate that," Rosinna said darkly.

"Do you know for sure? Do you know me at all? We've lived claw to claw for—how many years now? You still don't know when I'm joking and when I'm not."

"You can't be serious!" she cried. "This isn't a joking matter. If it's all gone, who pays the bills?"

"There's a little left for that, but any day now the papers will scream out the story of how Craggmoor is in bankruptcy and will be sold at public auction. Think of the riffraff that will come in here, into your precious mansion, and live like royalty. Doesn't it make your skin crawl?"

"I hate you! I truly do."

"I'm glad. It makes me feel warm inside."

"Tell me this minute you're lying!"

"Why should I?" He burst into laughter. "Would you believe me?"

"Stewart will surely die if you've lost his fortune."

"True again. Actually, what I've done is embezzle several million for myself."

"*That* I would believe."

"You would."

"If you won't tell me the facts then I will go to the accountant!"

"Why haven't you already?" Garth shouted. "If you're so worried, I'd think you'd have a weekly financial report in your money-grubbing little hand. Why bother me with this drivel, as you call so many things? The money isn't important to me. I made the funds available to the broker in New York. The accountant tells me how it's going. That's my job and I do it. That's all I do, despite your ugly suspicions that you enjoy so much. Stop your self-righteous act and start doing business like a sane adult."

"I just thought I'd ask you, as long as you were here." She shrugged her shoulders.

"Well, don't. I'm here about the business with Merri and for no other reason. My chief concern is to find my real sister, in one piece, if possible."

"And make scandalous advances with our houseguest while you're at it?"

"Ah! Now she's a houseguest. Last night she was an intruder, subject to an investigation and thorough police check. You make me laugh. I think it's time I left. I'm exhausted by your childish attempts to irritate me."

"Garth, wait. What do you think of that incident last night?"

"Nothing."

"Nothing? You think she made it up?"

"No. I mean, I'm not thinking about it at all. I don't *want* to think about what's going on here. The more years I hang around, the uglier things get. How should I know what really happened last night? Did you check on Jerry? Maybe he was playing cops and robbers."

"Stop it this instant! I won't let you speak of my brother that way. Jerome is a fine, sensitive man who minds his own business. He never would have…"

"See you later, Rosinna. Tell Florence I'll be back for

dinner. That should give you enough time to think up some new torments. I'll look forward to it."

"Your manners are despicable." Then she called again. "Garth, wait! Do you think we should really let this... this girl stay? We know nothing about her."

There was a long pause. "Intruder or houseguest? Make up your mind, Rosinna. I tell you, I don't know what happened last night. I don't think Merri does either. Still unconvinced?" Garth sighed. "You're hopeless. You're a suspicious old cat. I'm a little sick of your company just now—and I'm warning you. Be nice to her. You've already driven one Merry away. Don't do it again. I don't know what happened the day my sister left, but I do know you were the last to see her. Until she is found, I put all the blame on you."

"I had nothing to do with—"

"Didn't you, Rosinna? Your jealousy, your haughty disapproval of everything Merry ever did..."

"I was very fond of Merry."

Their voices seemed to be getting closer. Afraid I'd be caught eavesdropping, I turned back to the stairs.

Rosinna screamed as if in anger. "Garth!"

"Lies!"

I heard a struggle.

"The longer this goes on," he panted, "the more I fear for Merry. What's wrong with you? Aren't you worried, even a little? For all I know you chopped her up in little pieces and mailed her to China. She had controlling interest—"

"You can't be serious!"

"I am very serious. You're a poor liar. I'm certain you know where she is. So you watch it, Rosinna dear. I'll trip you yet. In the meantime, another suspicious episode like last night…If Merri gets hurt in any way…"

With a choking cry, Rosinna fled from the kitchen, her slippers clattering away.

I made a wild dash for my room. I would die if they saw me—after what I had heard. I pressed my door closed and leaned against it, wishing I could get a deep breath or quiet my heart. I couldn't wait to get away from Craggmoor! Every minute I stayed seemed to draw me deeper and deeper into a web of hate and suspicion and fear. I didn't even have to do anything. I was already involved and helpless, except to escape.

I heard a faint scream.

I froze, listening for more. It came softly, a cry, a moan from the end of the hall. I hadn't heard Rosinna come up the stairs, but I was sure the cries came from her room, and who else could it be but her? Unless…

I flung my door open and ran down the hall. The moans were coming from the same room I'd been in the night before. I was afraid to open the door, but I did without pausing. Rosinna lay sprawled on the floor, in front of a doorway that led to a narrow, enclosed stairway behind her. At the moment I reached her and helped her sit up, Florence, the plump cook, rushed up from below.

"What happened?" I cried.

"Nothing," Rosinna panted, straightening her torn dress. She pressed her hand to her chest and tried to get a deep breath. "I fell. I'm all right now."

"Anything I can do to help. Miss Rosinna?" Florence asked from behind. She held onto the railing tightly and threw a frightened look at me.

"Thank you, Florence. I'm fine. Go back to the kitchen." Rosinna got unsteadily to her feet. For a moment she let me support her. Florence nodded uncertainly and went back to the kitchen.

"How did you fall?" I asked.

Her eyes softened. She smiled weakly. "Don't look so worried." She pushed at tears still standing on her cheeks. Taking a deep breath, she pulled free of me and indicated the room, done in white brocade wallpaper and heavy lace curtains. "How do you like the morning room?"

So that's what it was.

"It's delightful to serve breakfast in," she said. "My mother used it often. We don't any more, as you can see. Now please, don't be upset. I often use the kitchen stairs. This time I was terribly angry about something Garth said to me. We were…discussing something—heatedly, as usual. I ran up in a blind rage, I'm afraid. It was a simple accident. I've never been known for my grace." As she spoke her eyes darted furtively around the sheet-shrouded room.

"This was the room I came into last night," I said. "I mistook it for your room. Remember, I wanted to tell you about my balcony door?"

Rosinna sighed. "It was nothing, Merri, really. You must have left it open yourself. You probably stumbled into a chair in here."

"I never opened the door and I sure didn't stumble. I came down the hall to tell you about the footprints on my carpet. I heard breathing and came in here. Someone grabbed me. He threatened me! He nearly suffocated me on that sofa there. He pushed and pushed…"

Rosinna walked awkwardly to the door, turned and waited for me to follow her out. I finally did, seeing that she wasn't going to believe my story, or wasn't going to *let* herself believe it.

"Rosinna, how did you fall?"

"I quite think I've explained enough."

We locked eyes for a moment. Finally I looked away.

"Forgive me, Merri. I'm such a terrible hostess," she said after I started down the hall.

"I'd like to have a bath before breakfast," I said looking back. "Do you have a hair blower I could borrow?"

"Merry had one, I believe. I'll look in her room."

Curious to see my cousin's bedroom, I followed Rosinna into a large room across the hall from the morning room. A little of the icy-gray lake at the north side of Craggmoor showed through the crack in the partially drawn pink velvet drapes.

The room glowed pink and rosy, as inviting as the inside of a huge warm flower. "I love this room," I said softly.

"Yes, Merry had very good taste," Rosinna commented.

Dominating the room was a massive mahogany four-poster that almost reached the ceiling. It was covered with a spread heavy with sheer ruffles. A giant white teddy bear lay on the lace-edged pillows. The room was decorated in white and shades of deep rose. Bright-colored toys and stuffed animals lined a wall of shelves. Across the room an expensive stereo, guitar, and skis were mute evidence that an active, lively girl had once enjoyed the room.

Rosinna went to the dressing table and took a hair blower from the drawer. I was wandering around the room marveling that not a speck of dust lay on any of the tables—yet Merry had supposedly been gone two years. A white leather-bound diary lay on the bedside table. I almost reached for it before I caught myself. I looked away casually.

"Can we come in here again later?" I asked.

Rosinna handed me the blower. Her expression was quite innocent but her eyes were guarded.

"If it wouldn't be too…nosy of me, I'd like to know what Merry took when she left. Is there any way of telling?" I edged away from the diary and ran my hand over an oil painting of a mountain lake that hung over her desk.

"It's been such a long time," Rosinna said halfheartedly.

"Maybe we could figure out where she went by what she took."

"I suppose I could deduce what is missing if I gave it some thought."

I didn't really care what Merry took, I just wanted to get my hands on that diary. I didn't for a minute suppose that Rosinna hadn't already read it all, but I was dying to know if Merry had left any clues—clues that Rosinna would never tell me, of all people.

Rosinna led me out the door and closed it carefully behind us. "After breakfast we'll look around. Garth said he'd be back later today. Maybe he'll show you the grounds."

"Then he's left already?" I asked, feeling devious. I knew full well he had.

"Oh, yes. A busy man like Garth mustn't waste his time. Excuse me please, Merri. I seem to have twisted my ankle and I'm going to soak it."

She went quickly to her room and almost slammed her door. I went back to the morning room and crouched at the stairway to examine the top step. The carpet was loose along the edge. She *might* have tripped…

As I headed back to my room I didn't let myself think about the other possibility.

• • •

The bath helped me relax. I dried my hair, and it turned out nicer than usual. I packed my suitcase and left it by the door. With my self-confidence and strength buoyed for what I assumed would be a difficult and awkward situation, I went down to breakfast.

I found Rosinna sitting at the oval table by the windows in the kitchen. From where she sat she had a terrific view of the courtyard. The sun was out. Melting snow ran off the roof in a steady dribble.

Rosinna, deep in thought, traced the lacy tablecloth pattern with her silver grapefruit spoon. When I came in, she looked up and smiled. The dark thoughts dulling her solemn gray eyes disappeared quickly.

Jerome appeared from the den to my left and nodded tersely. "Good morning, Merri." He held out his hand and, awkwardly, I realized he wanted me to shake it. For the moment my hand touched his I felt a disagreeable shudder run down my back. Shaking hands with Jerome was like holding a piece of raw meat! I crossed him off my mental list of middle-of-the-night attackers. I would have remembered *his* clammy touch. That left only Garth to take the blame—Garth Favor, with his hair-trigger temper and unreadable face.

"Good morning, Jerry." I smiled despite my churning thoughts.

"Jerome, if you please," he said curtly. He paused behind Rosinna's chair and gave her cheek a peck.

I just stood awkwardly while he sat and shook out his napkin.

"Please sit down," Rosinna said. "Coffee or tea?"

"Coffee, if it's no trouble."

"Not at all. Florence? Have we any coffee made?"

Florence poured me a cup right away and set it on my saucer. Her eyes sparkled with amusement, but in every other way she remained perfectly proper. I imagined Florence and Garth got along very well. The two of them probably had a wonderful time making sport of Rosinna and Jerome.

"How's your ankle?" I asked.

Rosinna looked startled. She glanced at Jerome casually and then smiled. "It was nothing."

"What's this?" Jerome scowled, eyeing me like an angry parrot.

"Nothing, Jerome," Rosinna assured him. "I simply twisted my ankle this morning and Merri was kind enough to ask after it."

"I'm glad it wasn't serious," I said perversely, knowing she was trying to pass the accident off lightly.

"Tell me what happened," he demanded.

Rosinna seemed to soften, becoming helplessly feminine. It was very much like how she had been with me right after her accident. I watched in fascination. It was as if she wanted—needed—sympathy!

Jerome leaned across the table trying to catch Rosinna's evasive eyes.

"I was...upset by something Garth said. When I went up to my room, I tripped on the stairs. We must replace that carpet...Jerome, I'm not hurt, really. My ankle is quite all right."

Jerome drew up inside himself, leaned back slowly, and reached for his teacup. Rosinna watched him breathlessly.

My hair prickled. Jerome's manner changed from extreme concern to sudden disinterest.

Rosinna seemed surprised and disappointed. Deliberately she relaxed her grip on her spoon and turned to me. "Now, isn't that just like a brother?" She laughed, covering the sudden hush. "He's upset that I fell, but finding that it was my own clumsiness, that I was merely angry with Garth, he's no longer concerned."

Jerome sipped stiffly as if he didn't wish to hear her. He kept his eyes from meeting mine. Neither the tilt of his pointed chin nor the angle of his thin eyebrows gave me a clue as to what he was thinking.

"Sometimes he's as bad as Garth," she muttered.

No wonder she was always so pleasantly surprised when I worried about her. She thought no one cared. Aunt Coral had had a philosophy about people like that. She used to say those who thought others cared nothing for them either cared little for themselves, or nothing about others.

"Neither of my brothers care about me," Rosinna went on sadly.

Jerome's hand trembled ever so slightly as he set down his cup. "Where *is* our dear stepbrother this morning?"

"Off to get his car pulled from the snow and back to work, I imagine." Rosinna sighed with boredom.

"Did you say he'd be back for dinner?" I asked, beginning my breakfast.

"Yes."

Jerome's cold eyes stared through me, making me shiver.

"How's Stewart this morning?" I asked.

Rosinna didn't answer right away. "I haven't been in to see him yet. I was resting."

"Of course," I said—but I wondered what mornings must be like for him.

"We'll visit with him before we go through Merry's room," Rosinna said.

"What on earth are you going to do that for?" Jerome coughed.

"Merri thinks we can locate her cousin simply by listing what she took when she left." Jerome stared at me as if I were crazy. The way Rosinna said it, it sounded like she thought my idea was dumb too. And that's just how I felt. Dumb.

"Is that really any of your business, Merri?"

"Did anybody else think of that?" I shot back.

"It's highly improbable..."

"But what if she took only warm clothes, or cool ones?"

Jerome smiled at me as if I were hopelessly stupid. I really felt like slapping him.

"You're right," I conceded, clenching my teeth. "It's a crazy idea and I have no business...I've decided I should—"

"Now, see what you've done?" Rosinna scolded. "You've offended her and she's only trying to help. Come now, Merri. If you're finished, let's go up to say good morning to Stewart."

We all got up at the same time. Jerome threw his napkin down and waited until I'd moved toward the door before he spoke to Rosinna in a whisper.

"Why shouldn't we go through her things?" Rosinna whispered back. "That's nonsense! Stop worrying. Maybe we'll find her yet. Merri could be exactly right."

Jerome looked absolutely furious. Rosinna didn't seem worried, though, so I didn't let it bother me.

We went around to the front staircase and started up.

Rosinna seemed to be favoring one ankle, though she was trying hard to hide it.

"Shouldn't you see a doctor about that?"

"What? Oh, it is a bit swollen now, isn't it? You're a terrible worrier, Merri. I'll be perfectly all right by tomorrow."

"Jerome thinks I'm nosy, doesn't he?"

"Of course not! He's just concerned that you're learning too much of our private matters. It's also for his protection that we lead quiet lives. He is quite widely published, but sensitive about it. He detests notoriety. Perhaps he fears you'll talk about us after you leave. I've assured him that's utter nonsense. You have an understandable interest in Merry's disappearance. Besides, you're hardly a stranger to us now. I feel as though you're part of our family."

I nearly stumbled.

"I explained about how very rude I was to you yesterday. Why, it hardly seems like just yesterday, does it? I didn't realize how much I've needed company. It's awfully nice having you here."

"I thought..."

"Oh, I'm sure you imagined I didn't want you to stay, but that's not so. I was merely being cautious. You must believe that I truly cared for Merry and want very much to find her."

"Then my idea isn't too dumb?"

"Not at all. Don't let Jerome frighten you. He's as gentle as a lamb. I don't know what I'd do without him. This whole affair has upset him as much as any of us. Only he doesn't want to admit it."

Then she knocked at Stewart's door. "Are you up yet?"

"Maybe we're too early."

"Nonsense. Stewart? Merri is here to see you."

The door flew open and Stewart stood there wild-eyed. When he saw me, his face fell. I knew who he wanted to see and it made me feel guilty. Maybe I was welcome, but I put him so much in mind of his daughter that it hurt him more than it helped.

He hadn't shaved or dressed. His dark hair stood out wildly and under his tragic eyes were deep circles. My heart reached out to him.

"What do you want?" he grumbled.

"Just by to say good morning," Rosinna said cheerfully, but I saw her eyes. She was disgusted and ashamed, even a little hurt that he wasn't glad to see her.

"Why don't you look over Merry's room while I talk to Stewart for a moment?" I suggested.

Rosinna nodded and marched away.

"Go away." Stewart sighed, turning away. "I'll talk to you later."

He took a huge gulp from his juice glass and grimaced. Already the smell of liquor filled his room. With his face gray and his hands trembling, I could see just how sick he really was. As I had overheard Garth say, it was a wonder Stewart was still walking around.

"Come and sit down," I urged gently. "How do you feel?"

"Terrible."

"Can I get you anything?"

He shook his head. It looked like it would drop off. He sank to the edge of his unmade bed. "Come back later, Merri. I don't like anyone seeing me like this."

He got up again painfully and went to the mirror. He ran his hands through his hair. The sadness in his eyes was bone deep.

"Looking at you, Stewart, makes me want to cry."

He turned and chuckled. "Me, too!" He went on laughing until it sounded more like sobs. "Every day I get up and say, Stewart, you bum, you can't drink today. When Baby comes back and sees you like this she'll be so disappointed. Then I think, maybe today will be the day. Today she'll call. Today she'll walk up the drive with that big smile. When she sees me, she'll come running. So I get dressed and shave and comb my hair. I stand by the window and wait. When the hours go by and my legs get tired, I say, 'Just one little drink to hold me till dark. Just a little one.' By evening I'm so smashed I don't care if she ever comes back."

I went to him and put my arms around his shoulders. He was so terribly thin. He shook when I touched him.

"Don't," he moaned.

"Don't be so sad, Stewart. I'll find her."

In the mirror, I watched his eyes fill with tears. His tired face broke into a faint, patient smile.

"Never give up hope. Merry loves you. She's coming back."

Trembling, he shook his head. "She's gone," he whispered thickly. "My baby's gone. She was so happy those last days. I was home from the hospital. We had the biggest Christmas ever. I bought her a car and new skis. I would have bought her two cars—two anything—just to make her happy. Then...poof! No more Merry. Rosinna said she was tired of our life, but I don't believe that. She was a Glenden. She liked money!"

"I'm going to do everything I can to find her," I insisted.

He shook off his tears and faced me, smiling bravely.

"You do that, if it makes you happy. I'll just get dressed now and see what I can see from the window. Maybe today…"

I watched him drift across the room mumbling sadly. I slipped out quietly and closed his door. My chest was tight. I needed someone to tell me how to be strong, to tell me everything would be all right for Stewart. Nobody could tell me that though. Nothing would ever be right for Stewart until he had his daughter back.

I shook off my own tears and hurried down the hall toward Merry's bedroom. Rosinna had opened the drapes and was waiting. "How's Stewart?" she asked, offhandedly.

I shrugged.

"Merri?"

"He's sad," I said, gulping down the rock-hard lump in my throat.

"Stewart's always sad. He just can't accept—"

"Have you noticed what's missing?" I interrupted. I couldn't stand another minute of her careless attitude.

"One suitcase from her matched set here. Lovely shade of red, aren't they? Several dresses—but I can't honestly tell what else. It's been so long now. She was always getting something new."

I nodded sadly. Then I remembered the diary. "Have you checked all her drawers?"

Sighing, Rosinna pulled out one and picked through the layers of sweaters halfheartedly.

I edged around the bed, intending to slip the diary under my arm. I patted the table behind my back as I watched Rosinna. When I felt nothing, I turned. It was gone!

"Is this how she left her room?" I asked, glancing behind me at the bare table. I looked around. It wasn't in sight.

"Yes, I haven't touched a thing. That would upset Stewart, you know," she said.

My mind raced in a dozen directions. Where was the diary?

I joined Rosinna in the closet, hoping she didn't notice my preoccupation. "What kind of dresses are gone?"

"Just a group from right here in the middle."

"She sure was neat." I laughed nervously. "My closet always looks like main street after a tornado."

Rosinna laughed. "She was untidy too. That comes from having someone else to do all the work. Jean does our things so nicely. I must admit I love having a maid. It's my only vice."

"Just four dresses gone? How about shoes? No jeans or pants outfits?" It did seem strange that she took so little.

"No, as a matter of fact. You see, I'm certain she took only these because Jean had just cleaned her room that very morning. I spoke to Merry right after lunch. When she left me, I assumed she went to see Stewart as she usually did. Later we all realized she was missing. I came in here to see if she was sleeping. I found her closet just like this."

"What kind of dresses were they?"

"I'm afraid I can't say. She had so much, as you can see."

I eyed the crowded closet enviously. "It's useless then. Did she have a favorite place? A ski resort maybe, or a friend..."

"I don't know," Rosinna said lightly. "She was a busy girl, in and out at all hours. I only saw her when she was with Stewart. When he was so ill, she stayed with him exclusively. I'm afraid I knew very little about my sister. I'm sorry I'm of so little help. You see, I'm not good at anything in particular.

Even my memory is poor."

Was that true? Someone like Rosinna ought to have known every stick and board in Craggmoor—every dress in Merry's closet, including those missing. She probably knew how much they cost and how many times each had been worn. Poor memory, huh?

"Don't be too disappointed," she said, noticing my frown. "We've been through this same torture ever since the day Merry left. Always the questions—why, where?"

My eyes strayed to the empty bedside table before Rosinna led me out and closed the door. Were the answers in that diary?

"Would you mind if I stayed in my room until lunch?" I said, suddenly tired and irritable. "I'm still awfully sleepy."

"Of course not. I'll send up a television later, if you'd like to watch."

I nodded and actually found myself yawning.

"I believe I'll get off this ankle and rest myself," she added. "I do think I've actually sprained it!"

It looked pretty bad to me, but I didn't say anything. I was tired of being put in my place.

My room had already been made up when I got back. I lay down on the cool flowered bedspread, trying to figure when I would get a chance to go through Merry's room— alone. What happened to my itch to leave? I wondered. Stewart. I couldn't leave him alone and at the mercy of Rosinna. She was just waiting for him to die so she could have his money.

The thing I couldn't figure was what happened to Merry. It would have been a stupid move for Rosinna to drive her away. Merry had controlling interest in her father's money.

Maybe Merry had been running for her life. Maybe she stopped only long enough to grab the first handful of clothes in her closet.

Four

"Where do you want the TV, m'lady?" came a voice that dissolved my restless dream.

I waved before opening my eyes. "Right over there."

"Ah ha! I've caught you! You've grown accustomed to servants already. For shame, Merri Glenden of Illinois. I thought you were made of sterner stuff."

I sat up blinking.

"You look pretty like that." Garth smiled mischievously, bent over a portable TV by my door. "Has anyone ever barged into your bedroom and told you that?"

I laughed weakly and rubbed the sleep from my eyes. "Do you barge into many bedrooms?"

"Got me there." He smiled, straightening. "Rosinna said you were resting. Feeling better?"

"Yes. Have I slept all day?"

"Only two hours. You've taken to our rich lazy ways quickly. You're not sick, are you?"

"No. Do I look it?"

"I was just worried after that incident last night—it's effect on you. That's why I came back so early."

He wore a luscious blue pullover that brought out the sparkle in his eyes. I did what I could to avoid the leap in my pulse, but it was useless. Everything about him was attractive, especially his devilish smile.

"I'll get along okay here," I said, sliding off the bed and fluffing my hair. I wished he would quit staring at me, but it was in his nature to tease. He knew he made me squirmy.

"Florence is fixing us a big pizza. We can talk everything over after you're properly nourished. Hungry?" he asked. He held out his hand and I took it.

His touch left me prickly with excitement. We stepped out into the hall and that was when I remembered bumping into him the night before. If he had been at this end of the hall, he couldn't have been in the morning room seconds before pressing me into that sofa with murderous brutality. At least I hoped Craggmoor wasn't infested with more secret passages. The kitchen stairs were bad enough.

"You're quiet," Garth said. "Is everything all right?"

"I think so. I didn't like that fall Rosinna took this morning. It could have been…" I was about to say fatal when Garth halted and grabbed my arm. "It might have been serious," I said hesitantly.

"What fall? I just talked to her and she didn't mention it."

Garth's face was totally innocent. How could I suspect that he pushed his stepsister? I had such an awful imagination. I was as suspicious as Rosinna and that made me feel awful.

"She fell at the top of the kitchen stairs—you know, back in the morning room—right after you left."

Garth's face wrinkled with dark thoughts. "Was

she hurt?"

"She twisted her ankle a little. I heard her cry out. After last night I was so jumpy I ran to see what happened. I found her lying on the floor in the morning room. She was scared! She won't admit it, but she's worried about last night too. Just because this is a fancy place, it's stupid to pretend nothing can go wrong in it." I watched his eyes closely. I was sure he knew nothing about Rosinna's accident.

"This place isn't usually so mysterious," Garth said, shaking his head. He forced a smile. "Actually, Craggmoor is dull. I'd sure like to know who grabbed you last night though. Jerry must have been lurking in the shadows drumming up excitement for one of his crummy novels. That's about his speed."

"I didn't know he was famous. I've never seen one of his books."

"Probably because he pays to have them published and the bookstores use them to prop up old shelves. He also uses a pen name—the family rep, you know."

"I know it wasn't Jerry," I said trying to hold back a giggle. Garth looked so fierce! "Jerry's hands are like…"

Garth raised his eyebrows embarrassingly. "He had his clammy hands on you already?"

I made a face. "We *shook* hands, this morning. Clammy, that's the word. I would have remembered hands like that."

"And Stewart couldn't hurt anyone," Garth added and started down the staircase. He rubbed his chin and scowled more and more deeply. Then he stopped and whirled, looking up into my face with an expression that made me feel like a villain. "You suspect me, don't you? That's why you're so distant. I'm cut to the quick!"

I looked away. Garth seemed to sag a little. His hand fell from the banister and flopped at his side. "Now I know how some of my clients feel, beaten before they've even tried to clear themselves."

"I'm sorry!" I said hastily, running down the stairs after him. "It's just that I overheard the argument you and Rosinna had this morning. Some of the things you said—"

"Just because Rosinna and I fight..." Garth erupted.

"That's just it, Garth. You don't just fight with her. You get downright cruel. She's not that bad!"

"Isn't she?" He shook himself and deliberately softened his face. "Sorry, I didn't mean to shout. You're right. I'm mean. The meaner I get, the better I like it. I bear grudges a long time. Rosinna has twisted the knife in my back plenty of times. I can't resist getting my digs in now that I'm a big boy. Rosinna's a lot older than me, you know. I'm only just now catching up. It feels good to be on top for a change."

"She doesn't look much—"

"Older?" Garth chuckled. "Dear, *I'm* twenty-six. Rosinna is beyond that by eight or nine years. Don't dare tell you know, or you'll feel the sharper side of her razor-blade personality. Rosinna's a shrewd old girl. I wouldn't be one bit surprised to learn she had Merry kidnapped. She's the kind that would burn the ransom note."

I shook my head and ignored him.

"Don't think the idea hasn't crossed my mind," he said, half laughing. "I wouldn't put anything past Rosinna."

"You really hate her?" I said playfully, but underneath I watched him as closely as I knew how.

"In a stepbrotherly sort of way." He grinned at himself.

"Did you chase her up those stairs then?"

My question really caught him by surprise. His cheeks flushed and his mouth worked helplessly. I felt uncomfortable and sorry I'd baited him that way. The hurt in his eyes made me cringe, but I just couldn't beat around the bush. I liked Garth—or rather, I wanted to. I tried to explain that to him. "I've got to trust you," I said, plucking at his arm shyly.

He sulked. Finally he met my eyes. "You think I'm that kind of guy, huh?"

"Wouldn't I be stupid if I blindly accepted everything you claimed to be? Somebody threatened me last night. This morning I hear an argument followed by a fall. Everybody acts so weird here, what am I supposed to think? I suspect everybody, but I ask you right out…"

"What's so suspicious about my sibling rivalry?" Garth asked, jutting out his chin.

"Not that exactly."

"What then?"

"The double messages. Which is truth, which are lies? Rosinna said this morning that I seemed like a member of the family to her, but I know that's just…"

"Glop."

My nervous burst of laughter broke the tension between us. "Right. I can't believe a word she says because I know she wishes she'd never set eyes on me. Honestly, Garth, sometimes you don't talk like a lawyer."

"That's because the first six years of a child's life are the formative ones. I spent those years under my poor mother's protective wing. Unfortunately, she had a lot of holes in it."

Boldly I tightened my grip on his arm. "Who else here have I got to trust? Just you. If you keep doing things that confuse me…"

"We've known each other less than a day," Garth pointed out. "I've tried to be honest. If I come off as a jerk…" He stopped and shook his head. "Hey, come on. Let's eat and get this mess ironed out. I promise, I won't keep anything from you. Ask away. But first, to answer that last bombshell, no, I did not follow Rosinna or push her *up* the stairs."

I paused. I ran the whole accident through my mind as it must have happened. "You couldn't have! Not *up!*"

He grinned and pulled me along to the kitchen. "I wish I won all my cases as easily."

Florence was just putting the pizza on the table. She gave Garth a loving pat on the arm as we sat down.

"I'll bet you didn't think Craggmoor could come up with something like this," Garth said, lifting up a wedge and grinning at the gooey cheese.

"It looks fantastic!" I said, feeling my mouth water.

"We're having lobster thermidor tonight, Rosinna's favorite," Garth said over a mouthful. "She sure wants to impress you."

"She has," I said, trying to be a little more mannerly and dabbing at my mouth with a linen napkin I hated to get dirty. "She confirms all my suspicions about her."

"Glad to hear it. What's she done now?"

"We went through Merry's room this morning—twice actually. I saw a diary and figured I'd sort of borrow it when she wasn't looking—to see if Merry left any clues. Quit looking at me like that. I'm not usually such a snoop. It's just that Stewart…"

"Enough excuses. Go on!"

"When I looked the second time, it was gone."

Garth nodded. "She's afraid you'll read about Merry's

numerous dates. I'm surprised you haven't noticed the distinct tinge of green around Rosinna's eyes. She's jealous. They don't use the term so much any more, but it fits her— old maid."

"Maybe Merry really did run away to get married," I said.

"Not without telling Stewart, she wouldn't. Besides, when did she have time for romance? She spent every day with Stewart. You know, I made a big mistake getting Stewart to sign his estate over to us—but there was so much involved. It had to be properly managed. I really thought Stewart wasn't going to make it. Even so, as much as there is left, there's no new money coming in. I don't expect Jerry to write any best sellers. Rosinna is too 'dignified' to work. Then there's me, but I barely pay the rent on my apartment. Merry might have snapped a rich guy if she'd tried—what I mean is, no new money. I had to do something. Craggmoor is expensive. It needs carefully budgeted finances and solid investments to keep it going. Stewart's not up to that any more, so I'm in charge. Merry got controlling interest to balance the three of us warring idiots. It wasn't so she'd get all the money. Rosinna and Jerry are so selfish they don't understand that. Rosinna wants her full quarter of the estate now so she can live in dignity. She doesn't realize how carefully we have to plan ahead. As for Jerry, he's just too stupid to manage money."

"The arrangements to preserve Craggmoor have done nothing but turn all of you against each other."

Garth rubbed his hands on the napkin and then pushed back his plate. He raised serious blue eyes to mine. "With Merry out of the way, that leaves the estate in thirds and upsets the balance."

"You think—"

"Something happened to Merry?" He paused and looked away. "Yes. If she is dead her nearest relative, namely Stewart, would inherit. That puts us back at the beginning again."

"Would Rosinna know that?"

He put his finger to his lips. "I don't know. All this time I've just been sitting on my hands hoping something would break. Maybe Merry really couldn't take Rosinna or Jerry or Craggmoor any more, which was possible."

"You haven't mentioned any of this to Stewart, have you?"

"Oh, no! Wouldn't dare. It'd kill him. Who knows? Maybe Rosinna planned it that way. Get rid of Merry and pretty soon Stewart would...Hell, Merri. I don't know if Rosinna'd do such a thing. It's just that I have to keep telling myself that something weird happened to her. She wouldn't have deserted Stewart. She wasn't that kind of girl."

"But it's been two years now. What have you done lately?"

"What would you have me do, climb Pikes Peak and call her? I grant you, I'm a lazy slob about the whole mess. I feel helpless and stupid, but I don't know what else to do. Who knows, maybe Rosinna was dumb enough to think she could have her share. She probably planned to talk Jerry into helping her out with his share—reduce me to a hired hack... What she didn't count on was Stewart surviving after all... and good ol' me. Legally, I've tied her hands. She can't touch the money. I figure if she knows anything at all she'll spill it when she wants that money bad enough."

"What would happen if you just let her have her share?"

"Rosinna would live lavishly, for five, even ten years. Jerry'd squander his publishing junk. But then Craggmoor would go—for good."

"I thought you hated Craggmoor. Let them lose it if they want."

"No, sorry if I've given you the wrong impression. I value Craggmoor. I just can't stand living here. Rosinna's phony manners, Jerry's irritating conceit—I hate that. Craggmoor itself has charm. When I was little I used to hide in the library. I read the old diaries and autobiographies. Craggmoor is a grand place, crammed with history. A lot of love and toil went into building this monstrous old place. It ought to stay in the family, for Stewart's sake and Merry's and all the old Glendens who once lived here. I'm not a blood Glenden, but I love this barn."

He seemed a bit embarrassed by his sudden sentimental feelings. I finished the last bites of my yummy pizza and watched Florence carry dusty champagne bottles into the kitchen. She lined them up beside the long-stemmed crystal, humming as she worked.

"Rosinna's planning quite a feast," Garth remarked absently, his eyes following Florence into the pantry where she did most of her work. "I'm glad I've had a chance to tell you this," he said.

"At least now I know why you told her the money was gone."

He grinned at himself again. "I had her going, didn't I?" Then he leveled a low-lidded stare at me. "My, my! You got an earful this morning."

The blood rose to my cheeks. Florence turned from dusting the bottles and I shrugged a little. She looked a little shocked.

"Merri…" Garth probed, winking at Florence.

"It was too good to miss," I said, trying not to smile. "After last night I didn't know what kind of place I was in. I was ready to run home as fast as I could, too. You can't blame me for thinking you pushed Rosinna after an argument like that, can you?"

"Garth wasn't even here when Miss Rosinna fell this morning," Florence blurted out. "Excuse me, Garth, but you two don't think I'm deaf. I heard that bit of teasing myself. You know darn well she can't take it. She's so serious. She went storming up those stairs, angry as I've ever seen her. I saw Garth go down to the tunnel, Merri. You don't really think my boy would hurt anyone, do you?" She patted Garth's shoulder and frowned at me. "I heard her struggling with the door. Sometimes it sticks. You know, this place is old and getting a bit neglected."

"Okay," Garth said, stopping her. "Thank you, witness for the defense."

My face sizzled.

"I took the tunnel to the garage, borrowed a car and drove to a gas station down the mountain. I was back maybe an hour later to get my car towed from the lot."

I waved my arms and laughed. "I'm sorry I brought it up again."

"It's all right. No one's told you about the tunnel or the garage yet. You were out in the hall getting your ears burnt. When I didn't come barging out you naturally assumed..."

I covered my ears. "I promise I'll never suspect you again!"

Garth reached for my hand and squeezed it. "I'm honest, Merri. So honest I won't let Rosinna play grand mistress of Craggmoor. She's not a queen. Blue blood has never impressed me."

Florence nodded in firm agreement.

"I didn't embezzle or squander the family fortune." Garth smiled. "In fact, since I was put in charge it's grown. I'm just too much of a brat to tell Rosinna that. I like to see her squirm. I didn't attack you last night, in case you still harbor any doubts. I was never a boy scout, but I am a nice guy, deep down—very deep."

"Who attacked you?" Florence interrupted.

We told her about the night before. She flapped her dust rag to cool her flushed face. "What's come over this place?"

"Have you noticed anything suspicious?" Garth asked her. "The only logical explanation is that someone broke in last night."

"An open door, footsteps…anything," I put in, eager to hear if she knew anything. Just having her believe me would be a help.

"I swear." She smiled uneasily. "Ever since poor Merry run off…"

"Did she, do you think?" I asked.

She shook her head. "I don't know." She pulled out a chair and sat with us, leaning close to whisper. "I figured she went out through the garage and up the back road to the highway. That's what I told the detective."

"That's the only way out except for the main gate," Garth told me. "Somebody would have had to push the button to unlock it. As far as we know, no one did. There was no snow on the ground, so, no footprints. Any evidence was later covered by a heavy snowfall that night."

"I went to my room to rest," Florence said. "You'd think I would've heard her if she went out the back, but I sleep like the dead."

"Jerry was in his room working. Rosinna was...doing whatever amuses her, I guess," Garth said.

"What did Rosinna tell everyone?" I asked.

"She said she was having tea after lunch. Merry came in from somewhere, skiing, skating—I've forgotten. She talked to Rosinna and then went up to see Stewart. She never got there. Everyone agreed that Merry snuck out, disappeared, what-have-you, early that afternoon."

"Where were you?" I asked.

"I, my dear? I was working at my office in town oblivious of the tragedy in progress."

"Tragedy?" Florence gasped, fraying the edge of her dust rag.

"Disappearance," he corrected hastily. "If she left of her own free will, she broke Stewart's heart. That's a tragedy, I think. If she didn't..."

"Oh, please," Florence cried. "I wish it was all over and done with."

"Come on," Garth said, getting up. "I'll show you the tunnel."

I followed Garth down the second flight of kitchen stairs leaving Florence muttering unhappily to herself. We came out in a broad hall below the kitchen. The walls were bare stone and gave off a clammy, damp smell. Along the flagstone floor ran a blue and tan runner, worn with the years and dotted with lots of muddy footprints.

"In that room are the wines," Garth said, pointing to one of the many doors along the tunnel. "Over here, the larder. We used to play pirate in there. Down here is the furnace room—tool room next door."

I squinted at the bare light bulbs overhead. The raw light left no sinister shadows to feed my imagination. I was disappointed and found the tour boring.

"In here, under the ballroom, are the women servants' quarters. There's a storage room back of all that for decorations and chairs—parties, you know. A small elevator used to come in handy moving trunks up to the second floor guest rooms, but it's out of service now. No one ever visits. Most of this 'stately old mansion' looks the same as the morning room, shrouded in white, waiting for someone to bring it back to life. Ah! I'm beginning to sound like Rosinna! Shame on me. Anyway, the maids' rooms are nice. I used to visit down here a lot, not being of the upper crust, you know. It didn't bother me to associate with the help. The small windows overlook the gardens—great view. Overhead of us now is the road that passes the ballroom portico."

"I'm dying to see that."

"Rosinna didn't show you yet? How careless of her. I'll show you tonight. At the end of this tunnel, through those doors, is the garage. No less than five cars!" He smirked. "And over the garage is the gardener's house. There are extra rooms for the summer dirt boys. It takes about five to keep up the lawns in the summer. And believe me, they work night and day. Yep, Craggmoor is quite the joint."

"Nothing but an ordinary basement." I sighed.

"You imagined grease torches and shadows, maybe some rats along the walls...and secret rooms." He chuckled.

"It would have been charming."

"This was my favorite part of Craggmoor. I used to unscrew the light bulbs and play down here in the dark—that is, until Jerry got the idea he was going to play too.

The attic is fantastic too. I should take you up there. Trunks, books, magazines, newspapers, furniture—even the original Merrisa's wedding gown."

"When can we go up?"

Garth smiled and put his arm around my shoulder. "Merry wanted to wear that dress when she found the right guy. If I remember right, even the blueprints are up there, and Clinton's pickax that struck the fateful vein of gold."

"I'd love it."

Garth turned to me. "It would have been fun to have you here, years ago. Maybe the pirate would have won a few battles."

"Was it bad without me?"

"Very bad. Jerry always won. He and Rosinna liked to lock me in the larder. I'd eat myself into a stupor out of sheer revenge. Then I'd cry. I'm a proud man and was a prouder boy. I never begged to be let out. They wouldn't have anyway. I can still hear Merry padding down the tunnel in her pink coveralls sucking on the key. I think that's what made her such a fearless little fool. She thought she was queen bee because she could save her big brother."

"I wonder how they'd like being locked in there right now!"

He hugged my shoulders and then let me go. "I'm fond of my grudges—my one failing. I don't care to give them up, just yet."

He paused, with a secret inner glint in his eyes. I watched his face as he remembered those bitter times and had to force myself not to reach up and smooth away the lines around his mouth.

Suddenly he snapped his fingers. "I almost forgot!

I've got a surprise for you." I let him pull me along toward the stairs. "Are you too well brought up to accept presents from gentlemen?" he asked. "I'm perfectly honorable, I assure you."

I was panting when we reached the kitchen.

"Now, where is it?" he grumbled impatiently. "Rosinna? Where did you put it?" He kept shouting until Rosinna appeared at the top of the stairs.

"What is it? What's happened now?" she cried.

"Where's the box I brought?"

"Oh, really, Garth! I put it in the closet. You're so helpless."

"Sorry to disturb you. Toddle on back to your room and continue your witchcraft."

"Did you rest well?" Rosinna asked me, ignoring Garth.

"I feel fine now."

Garth pulled a large flat box from the closet and handed it to me, his eyes twinkling with excitement.

When I opened it I couldn't help let out a squeal. It was a gorgeous fur jacket made of several shades of white and brown jumbled together. It was so silky soft I put my face to it.

"You like it." He rocked proudly on his heels.

"Is this for me?"

"Since you were almost blue in your own coat yesterday, I decided you needed something warmer. I want to show you the grounds and promenade." He looked delighted as he took the jacket from me and held it open while I slipped my arms into the sleeves.

"I love it! But..."

"You couldn't possibly accept it."

I pulled it closed and spun around.

"You'd be forever in my debt. Perhaps I'd take undue advantage." His eyes flashed.

"You sound like something out of an old novel." I laughed. "Too late! I won't give it back."

"Think warmly of me?"

I smiled. "Thank you."

Above us Rosinna watched. As Garth got his coat, I saw her slip out of sight. The look in her eyes made me feel suddenly cold.

Garth showed me the gardens first. Winding paths, icy urns and perfect hedges gave me a frozen idea of what it looked like in bloom.

"I've got to paint this." I sighed. "Look at the way the mountain shows between those pines. The composition is perfect."

"I doubt they make enough white paint."

"Not now! In the summer! And I want to sketch the view from over there." I pointed to the semicircular lawn.

"The promenade. You have good taste. I'll show you the view."

Garth took my hand. His was warm and firm against my fingers. His touch left me tingling and eager to be as far as possible from Rosinna's jealous stare.

We scuffed through calf-deep snow along a path that followed the contour of a sheer cliff on our right. When we came out below the low wall ahead of us was the curve of the promenade.

Once we looked over the two-foot-thick stone wall it was like being on top of the world. Crags and ravines offset the sheer stone face. Beyond that stretched the plush residential area of Colorado Springs.

I turned and gazed back at Craggmoor. The lawn, the small wall, the drive, the fountains, the terraced steps and then the building—it all looked too fabulous to be real.

"This would make quite a picture too, wouldn't it?" Garth said.

"Craggmoor is truly magnificent." I sighed. I turned back to the view of the city and leaned my elbows on the wall to peer over the edge. "Who designed this wall?"

"The whole place is modeled after some palace in Germany, from what Clinton wrote in his diary. The wall and promenade are supposed to be like a battlement. It's not the best feature of Craggmoor though. For years the spring thaw left tons of water here. This whole section would have given way eventually."

I eased back from the edge.

"Nothing to worry about now." He laughed. "The landscapers figured a way to save the promenade. See the clump of bushes there in the middle? They disguise a drainage system that carries the water down below the wall. See where all the ice is?"

I looked over the side again. Far below a cascade of ice hugged the rocks.

"In spring people call it Craggmoor Falls. I can see it from my apartment. Most of the water comes from the side drains, there by the cliff. There's a couple more over this way." He pointed out the barely visible gratings beneath the snow. "It's frozen now," he said, "and they're ugly, but this spring they'll save Craggmoor."

I leaned back against the wall and smiled slyly. "You really love the place."

"I shouldn't. It's pretentious."

"I like it."

"I'm glad—but then, I think you'd like anything—and anyone…"

"You mean Rosinna."

"Yes, my dear stepsister."

"Let's not talk about her."

"You're right. She puts me in a bad mood. What I want to know is, how long are you going to stay? A week?"

"No…"

"If I don't move fast, you'll escape back to Illinois and I'll never see you again."

"Your timing seems fine to me."

"What *are* your plans? For the future, I mean."

"I want to finish art school."

He put his hand on my cheek. "You're red. Is it the cold? Could anyone talk you into staying after last night? Say, until spring when the garden blooms?"

He bent slowly, his eyes intense and his face suddenly soft and serious. He kissed me slowly. I wanted to wind my arms around his neck and never let go.

"Sh-h-h," he said as I tried to speak. "I'm trying to convince you. Stay, dear cousin. Stay near me."

He kissed me a little harder and I felt deliciously warm and happy. How this could have happened so suddenly and so completely, I didn't know, but it didn't seem to matter.

He pulled away and raised his eyebrows in a question, a hopeful one.

I started to smile. "I've already decided to stay. Didn't I tell you?"

Garth's eyes twinkled. "No wonder I'm such a good lawyer." Then he scowled. "What do you mean, you already decided?"

"I'm going to look after Stewart the way Merry did."

Garth pouted handsomely. "And what about you and me?"

"Why, I hardly know you, sir!"

"That can be changed!" He grabbed me and pulled me so close our noses touched. "I want you to stay because of me."

"You don't need me. Stewart does."

"Don't I?" He sighed and kissed me lightly. "I know a pirate who needs you to help him win battles. You can't help Stewart."

"You don't like to share, do you?"

"Don't make me sound more juvenile than I already am. Be advised you've cut me to the quick again."

I chuckled a little. "I like you very much."

He seemed about to speak and then held his tongue.

We started back toward the drive. When we crossed it and climbed the steps, I stopped him. "You're angry!"

"It's this business between me and Rosinna that keeps you from trusting me, isn't it?"

"Not that again!"

He made an impatient face. We walked around toward the lake. Garth paused and looked over the low wall at the dull, lumpy ice. He laughed. "I'm acting like a kid."

"You want me to say I'll stay because of you. All right, I am. I *do* like you. I was just being honest. You should appreciate that."

"Rub salt into my wounds. It's kinder."

"Garth," I said, putting my hand on his arm. "I've stopped suspecting you."

"I'm the only likely one."

"There's someone else in the house."

"Repeat that often enough, you may begin to believe it. Nobody could get past the security system. Until I prove myself innocent I will remain guilty."

"There *is* someone else, someone who wants to know where Merry is even more than I do."

Garth lounged against the wall. He stared thoughtfully at the north face of Craggmoor. "If there is someone lurking around here, you shouldn't stay and I shouldn't try to persuade you."

I slid my arm through his. "I will stay. I'm sorry I hurt your feelings."

"Dear girl, I have none."

"It's just that I decided this morning—"

"Enough! Let's get away from this dismal lake. It makes me nervous."

"More bad memories?"

"I nearly drowned in it one summer. Jerry's a rotten swimmer. After he pushed me in he tried to save me. He nearly choked me. I wound up saving him. Ah, the heroic stories I could tell you!"

"The way you feel about each other, it's a wonder you four kids survived this long." I laughed, trying to picture Garth and Jerome as skinny boys thrashing around in that gloomy water.

"One of us hasn't."

I looked at the ice and wondered what might lie under it.

"The police dragged the lake, combed the grounds, and searched the house. They went over this mountain and the whole city without missing a spot. No one saw her. No one offered her a ride. She never bought a ticket to anywhere..."

"She left with someone!" I said. "That's why the diary is gone! Rosinna knows who she left with."

"Sorry, dear. I read that diary in all its innocence. She hadn't written in it since she was fifteen. I still say Merry would not have willingly deserted Stewart for any reason—unless..."

"I won't believe she's dead! I can't lose her before I find her!"

He gave me a quick hug. "You're nice."

We just rounded the back of Craggmoor. From the courtyard we stared up at its inner walls.

"There's your balcony." He pointed to a row of balconies on the second floor, each separated by twenty feet or more and an outcropping of decorative stone. "The next one over is mine. The third is off an unused guest room." There was nothing below the balconies that a man could climb on.

"What's upstairs in that wing?" I pointed to the south section over the ballroom.

"Guest rooms and Jerry's studio. That skylight gets the north light and all that."

"Why is his room away from everyone else's?"

"Just his style."

"Nobody could climb to the balconies." I sighed, turning away. "I can't figure out..." I did see footprints on my carpet, I assured myself. "Someone must have been hiding on it." I shuddered. "Jerome left the dining room first, didn't he?"

106

Garth shrugged. "I think all the evidence keeps pointing to me. Maybe I swung across like a cat burglar. Hey, I'm kidding!" He gave me another quick squeeze.

"Maybe you'd better call the police."

"No," Garth said softly. "Something's going to break. The police can come after *I've* figured it out."

"Jerome wouldn't know anything, would he?" I asked. "I honestly don't think he's too smart—not smart enough to do anything to Merry anyway."

"He's weird enough, but he had no motive. Rosinna's the one with motive."

"We can be certain Stewart wouldn't have…"

Garth moved a few steps away from me. He looked like he was struggling and finally made a difficult decision. He turned to me and I didn't like the gray look to his face at all.

"Suppose Stewart took a drink the day Merry disappeared? He hadn't touched a drop for weeks and Merry was convinced he was finally off the stuff. Stewart is no mild-mannered pussycat when he's drunk. I know he's been nice to you, but his tongue's as sharp as Rosinna's. Before Natalie died he was a shrewd businessman—he was like that when he was drunk, in command. We didn't argue with him—and Merry, most of all, didn't like him when he was like that. We're all hotheads. Merry laid down the law. No more booze. If he slipped, had a drink that day, Merry would have been mad enough to—"

"You can't really think that's what happened!"

"No, it's just another possibility. I think it's a lot more probable than some of my other theories. I never told anyone though, until now."

"Would he have told her to leave?" I asked weakly. "Not

out of anger, but out of shame?"

"He might have. Or she might have said, forget it. She was giving up. Now, either she won't come back, or can't. End of mystery."

"He's kept on drinking because it doesn't matter any more," I cried. "Oh, Garth, it can't be true!"

We reached the front door and he pulled it open for me. Rosinna was just coming down the stairs as we went in. Seeing us together, she looked annoyed. "You look frozen." She smiled stiffly.

Garth helped me with my coat. "Coffee?"

I hesitated. I had to think. I had to be alone. "Not right now. I need to change my shoes. I'll be down in a minute."

Garth's theory about Stewart and Merry really threw me. My muscles felt like taut rubber bands. I tried to imagine Stewart driving Merry away with his drinking or Merry leaving out of anger. No, they couldn't! They loved each other in a way I envied. Their devotion was beautiful and tragic. I hated the thought that their last moments together might have been filled with anger.

My head ached as if it were filled with numbing ice cubes. Craggmoor was driving me nuts. Maybe it had driven Merry nuts, too. How she stood the rivalry and bickering I couldn't imagine.

I sank to my bed in exhaustion. That was it. Garth was right. It was the most probable theory. Merry either left willingly, out of anger, or Stewart told her to go. There was no more reason for me to stay. On the contrary, that was a very strong reason to go. I couldn't ignore that, or put it off. Despite my growing affection for Garth, I had to escape Craggmoor.

How could I explain it to Garth? He'd trusted me with his most painful theory and I turned around and...

Just then, my eyes fell to the faint marks on my carpet. Garth's theory was probable, but it didn't explain the person who grabbed me and demanded to know where my cousin was. Was Garth maybe the craftiest of them all, playing with my ignorance to throw me off from the truth?

Garth made me suspect Jerome, a self-centered but harmless fool. He pointed the finger at Rosinna and accused her of everything from kidnapping to murder. Now he placed the blame on Stewart.

Skillfully he argued every bit of evidence against himself—always ready with a handy excuse or bit of nostalgia from his embittered past to win me over. If he felt he had to defend himself so often, wasn't it because he was in some way guilty—protesting too much, as they say?

Angry tears stung my eyes. I'd trusted him. I'd ignored every instinct I had and trusted that snake! I'd even kissed him and longed for more! I was a fool.

The minutes ticked by, yet I knew I didn't yet trust myself to go down and face Garth. Maybe *I* could sneak out of Craggmoor and forget I ever came. How I wished I'd never looked at the papers in Aunt Coral's trunk!

I was still wondering why I had tried to make all this my business when Garth called through my door sometime later. "Rosinna's serving cocktails. Shall I save you one?"

I cleared my throat and dashed away my tears. "In a little while."

I relaxed my fists and wondered if I would make it through dinner. Food! My stomach turned. I reached for the phone beside my bed to call a taxi. I *would* sneak away, right down the back stairs and...

"Merri?" Garth stuck his head in my door.

I jerked around so he wouldn't see my face, grabbed a tissue instead of the phone and blew my nose.

"For crying out loud, what's happened now?" he barked. He came in and closed the door behind him.

"Not now, Garth."

"What's wrong?"

"I'm tired," I snapped. "Tired of being frightened. Tired of suspecting everyone. Ever since I came here I've felt nothing but confusion. Leave me alone. I need to think."

"But, why the tears?"

"Why not? If it amuses me."

"That sounds like good old Rosinna sarcasm to me." He stopped short and jammed his fists in his pockets.

"That's what it takes around here, isn't it?"

He started forward and reached out. I closed my eyes.

"Don't, Garth. I want to be alone. I'll be down for dinner later. Right now I just want to sit and pretend I'm back home."

"Is that why you get so upset when I suggest Merry's dead? You're still in shock over your aunt's death?"

"Yes! No—I don't know! It's that theory of yours about Stewart and Merry."

"I just suggested they might have quarreled."

"I don't want to believe anything like that."

"Why not? Stewart isn't a poor old saint. He's an alcoholic."

"Stop it!"

"What is it with you and Stewart?" Garth exclaimed angrily. "Stewart's got his faults just like the rest of us. I know you like him. So do I, but you can't close your eyes to—"

"Leave me alone!"

"I don't like to see you this way. I don't understand what happened."

"You started it. You've made me suspect Stewart. I wanted to help him. Now there's nothing left. I'm better off leaving."

"You thought Stewart could take your aunt's place?"

"You wouldn't know how it feels to lose someone you loved. Aunt Coral was all I had!"

Garth turned away. "I lost my mother, didn't I? You're not the only one who feels lonely and friendless, Merri."

I brushed away my tears. "I'm sorry. That was thoughtless of me."

"I grew up just as alone as you," he said softly. "Only I had no kindly aunt to soothe the pain. In a family like this… years in schools where I never fit in. I hated the stinking rich boys and they hated me. Sorry I've spoiled your pretty dream that Stewart is your new father, but God's truth is, I don't care. I don't want you turning all your attention to him like Merry did. You'll get caught up in his private hell."

"You're cruel."

"Maybe I am, Merri, but at least my eyes are open. I see my own faults as well as those of others. Believe it or not, I see a glaring fault in you. Your corn-fed beauty and Aunt-Coral innocence can't hide how childish you are. People are not to be trusted. Some are evil and that's a fact of life I'm sorry to have to tell you."

"Are you finished?"

"Yes, dammit!" He stomped to the door and flung it open. "Go ahead and leave—now, if you want. Or tomorrow morning, or whenever it amuses you. I'll stay to help you if any more 'prowlers' jump out of the shadows, but after you go I won't be around. You'll have to fight for yourself."

"It's philosophies like yours..."

"That help people survive," Garth finished for me. "Someday when you've grown up we'll see what you think of my philosophies. The only trouble will be that then all the things I love about you will be gone."

His words echoed down the hall and were followed by silence. "I'm sorry, Merri," he said more softly. "You seem to stir something in me I've never felt before. Please don't go just yet. Stay for dinner. I promise I won't say a thing to upset you."

He started to close the door. I heard the whisper of Rosinna's dress as she marched up the stairs.

"Garth, you absolutely appall me! What has possessed you?"

"If you say one more word, Rosinna, I swear I'll break your neck!" He slammed the door to his room and then all was quiet.

I folded up on my bed and cried. Rosinna discreetly closed my door. At last I was alone, alone to hear Garth's words ring in my ears.

Stewart tapped lightly at my door an hour later. Dinner was ready. I didn't want to get up. I felt drained and weak, too weak to avoid getting sucked deeper into their troubled lives. I was ashamed too, ashamed of myself and what they must have heard.

Garth was right. I was childish. The closer I got to the truth the more I wanted to hide from it. I only wanted to find Merry if it turned out to be romantic. If she met with tragedy, I wanted to pretend it hadn't happened.

At last I got up and washed and put on my best dress. Looking as presentable as I was going to get, I went downstairs with my head high.

When I entered the dining room they all rose and greeted me. We ate a delicious meal and chatted about harmless things. It pleased Rosinna to have it go so well. Stewart seemed happy. Jerome ignored us, as usual. Garth kept his promise and didn't say a word.

But under the smiles and polite words seethed the thoughts and suspicions that were a way of life at Craggmoor—and in a very short time had become a way of life for me.

Five

The next morning I woke to the wind swooping down the mountainside and beating against my window. It frightened me at first. I thought someone was trying to get in. As I poked my nose from under the blankets I felt the terrible cold in my room.

The room was so cold I almost expected to see my breath. Finally I slipped from the bed and hurried into the bathroom to huddle under the heat lamp in the ceiling. I dressed warmly, spent a long time fussing over my hair, and then finally couldn't put it off any longer.

I must have looked grim as I went down for breakfast a few minutes later.

"You don't look very rested," Rosinna said, seated at the kitchen table, immaculately dressed as usual. I wondered how she could look so calm. My nerves were so frayed I jumped every time a gust of wind struck the windows. A whisper of cold came from the frosty glass.

I rubbed my fingers together. "It's a little cold," I said.

"I can't imagine what the trouble is, Merri. I'm terribly sorry. We've never been completely without heat before. I hope you'll forgive the inconvenience. The furnace stopped during the night."

Jerome joined us. "It's deadly in here."

My eyes went right to his scrawny neck. He was so comically out of proportion—too little head for such wide, sharp shoulders, too much body for such small feet.

"How are you this morning?" he asked, interrupting my stare.

"Cold, but otherwise pretty good."

"Garth was terribly rude to you last evening," Rosinna injected bluntly, her eyebrows raised, her gray eyes calmly half-closed. "I can't imagine what provoked him."

"We're really getting on each other's nerves," I said. "I don't know just what it is."

"He behaved decently enough at dinner," Jerome commented. With a neat tap he lopped off the top of his soft-boiled egg. The silver egg cup teetered on the plate. I got the distinct impression he'd just beheaded his breakfast.

Florence scowled as she set hot chocolate and toast before me. She didn't like us discussing Garth.

"Garth knows his manners," Rosinna went on. "But sometimes he doesn't choose to use them. His true character shows through everything he does."

I prickled with indignation. Then I forced myself to ignore her veiled attacks. I wasn't going to care the least bit what she said about Garth.

"Is it true he asked you to leave?" Jerome inquired nonchalantly, peering over his fork with icy-blue eyes. "I didn't hear the conversation myself, you understand. I was in my studio."

"No, he—"

"Terribly rude." Rosinna sniffed. "I apologize for him."

"That's not necessary!" I snapped.

"You're very patient with him." Rosinna smiled. "Much more so than I."

My blood boiled. "The argument was my fault," I said.

"Of course, dear. Whatever you say. Actually, for being raised in the country, you've acquired manners I quite admire. You surely do have Glenden blood. Garth could take lessons from you."

I felt like stabbing her with my fork. The cat. No wonder Garth was so cynical. I couldn't really blame him for thinking I was foolish to place my trust in people I hardly knew. As for Rosinna, I'd *never* trust her!

"Is Stewart coming down soon?" I asked.

"For breakfast? Oh, no." She laughed softly. "I thought you realized Father takes his breakfast in his room. It's either generously laced tomato or orange juice. Which, Florence? I've forgotten."

Yanking her sweater around her shoulders, Florence conveniently left the kitchen.

"Why, where did that woman disappear to?" Rosinna exclaimed. She sighed with exasperation.

"Has Rosinna shown you the gallery?" Jerome asked. "Oh dear, she hasn't? Well, you simply must see it. My best paintings hang there. Don't you think so, Rosinna? We must show her right away. Let's go now."

"Not now, Jerome. We've hardly finished our breakfast. And I have a headache from this cold. Whatever is keeping Garth? He said repairing the furnace would take only a moment."

I looked up in surprise. I had thought Garth had left.

"What does he know of furnaces?" Jerry sniffed, dabbing his chalky lips with his napkin. "What an absurd idea, sending him to fix it."

I gulped the last of my hot chocolate and wished for more. "Where did Florence go?"

"I'm sure I don't know." Rosinna smiled. "She does many little chores around here, especially today on Jean's day off."

"When did Jean leave?" Jerome asked, jutting his head forward so he looked a lot like a chicken.

"This morning, I suppose. Surely the snow prevented her from leaving last night. Of course, I wouldn't know for sure. She comes and goes as it suits her. I suppose Florence went up to do the bedrooms."

I got up and poured myself more chocolate. Their eyes followed me disapprovingly.

"Then Garth must have driven Jean into town," Jerry said.

"Whatever for?" Rosinna cried.

"Why not? He obviously couldn't fix the furnace. So he's left, just when we need him, too. He's gone off with the maid and left us to freeze." He chuckled and left the table. "I believe the maid and her cowlike personality just suit him."

"Jean is a good maid." Rosinna sniffed. She got up from the table too. "Merri, would you care to see Jerome's gallery now? He'd be delighted to show you."

I smiled skillfully. "I'll just finish my hot chocolate. I'm cold to my bones."

She nodded, her eyes flicking over me critically. She

sure felt confident that morning, unlike the day before when she'd been upset and defensive. Maybe it was because Garth was gone. She could assume her superior role.

Garth could reduce her in a word. Without him, she was again the stately Craggmoor mistress. She enjoyed treating me like a child. I was glad when she and Jerome left the kitchen. My shoulders relaxed. I realized that I had been hunched over the table as they talked. My bones ached with cold and tension. It would be so good to get out of there!

I was finishing my second cup of chocolate when Florence returned from the tunnel. She began clearing the table, avoiding my eyes.

"Would you like something more?" she finally asked.

"No, thanks."

She nodded and carried the dishes into the pantry. She ran water and clattered pots around in the sink. Her forehead and the bridge of her nose met in a frown.

"Do you know how much longer Garth will be?" I asked, leaning in the doorway.

She turned and her expression eased a bit. "He's been gone for over an hour."

"Does it take long to fix the furnace?"

She shrugged. "As long as I've worked here, it's never broken down."

I sighed.

"Actually, Miss Merri, I was just down there to check on him. He's not there, so I guess they were right. He must have given up and left."

"Wouldn't he have said good-bye? Or mentioned when he'd be back?"

"He wasn't in much of a mood this morning. I'm not

118

sure he even meant to fix the furnace. He may have just wanted an excuse to leave."

"It's all my fault," I said. "I said some stupid things last night."

Florence's face softened more. "Garth's proud. You realize that. I've worked here many years. He's grown from a sullen, rebellious boy into a fine young man. But his temper...I try to tell him, but he won't listen."

"We had a terrible argument yesterday. We were talking about Stewart and Merry. He told me something that had bothered him a long time. I just couldn't accept it. Before I knew it we were shouting."

She nodded, her mouth in a sympathetic pout.

"I just wanted to tell him...I'm sorry."

"That's nice, Merri." She smiled. "Maybe he'll be back soon. I'll bet he went for the repairman. When he gets back I'll tell him you want to see him."

"Thanks, Florence."

"You look so cold. Better put on a sweater."

"I didn't bring one."

She wiped her hands and came to me. "Ask Rosinna for one," she said patting my shoulder.

"I'd rather not."

"Do you want to borrow one of mine? I wouldn't mind if you don't."

"Oh, Florence..." I sighed. "I wouldn't at all. Is it like this here all the time?"

"Like what, dear?"

"All the proper talk covering up so much anger and contempt?"

"It must sound dreadful to a stranger. You mustn't let

Rosinna or young Jerome trouble you. They don't have much to keep themselves out of mischief. Sticking their noses in the air is just their way of amusing each other. They mean no real harm. I admit they make me mad picking on Garth, but nothing I can do will change things. That Garth. He's like my own son. I worry about him."

"About Garth?" I giggled.

"Oh, yes. He can match words with anyone, but underneath he's a softy."

"I keep saying the wrong things."

"Don't you worry." She smiled. "I can tell you like each other. That pleases me. Sometimes it just takes a fella and a girl a while to get on the same track. just you wait. Before you know it, you'll both be running in the same direction. Then you'll say all the right things."

"You make me feel a lot better. You're a lot like my aunt. She always knew the right things to say."

"I'm honored you think so, Miss Merri."

"Please don't call me that. It sounds so fancy. I don't feel fancy at all today. I feel like a country bumpkin."

Florence laughed.

"I do! I don't even know how to eat an egg out of a silver cup. Isn't that awful?"

"Don't be silly, Merri! Eating soft-boiled eggs is no great accomplishment. It takes years of doing nothing else—and let me tell you, that's just about all that poor boy Jerome can do. I've been serving him soft-boiled eggs for so many years now I'm surprised he hasn't turned into one!"

I burst out laughing.

"That's one of Garth's jokes," she whispered.

She led the way down the stairs. "Dear me! I do love

that young man," she added. "I can't understand why he hasn't found himself a pretty wife to make him happy. He's so lonely, living by himself. Poor dear. He was so hurt when he mother passed on. Then his sister...missing all this time. I don't know how he holds up. We've all tried to put it from our minds, but not Garth. He'll never give up. He'll probably keep the detective on the case...forever. And regular as clockwork he comes up here to check on Stewart. He's real fond of his stepfather. The both of them just doted on Merry. I know Garth wasn't so worried when she was first gone. He kept saying he was glad she'd finally broken free— if that's what she did."

I followed her into the servants' hall. Just as we were opening the door, Florence nearly stumbled over the threshold.

"It's dark down here today," I said, grabbing her arm to lend her support. I looked around at the new, unfamiliar shadows. Without Garth's company and humor the tunnel was suddenly a frightening, murky place.

"I've got to remember to have Garth replace these bulbs," she said. "They just burned out this morning. Craggmoor's falling apart."

"Does Garth do all the handyman's work?"

"He shouldn't," she said sharply. She opened her door. "But with no male help since Tom, Garth is all we have. He doesn't mind, of course, but it isn't his duty."

"Jerome could do some things, couldn't he?"

"Why, I wouldn't ask Jerome to dust under a bed! He's the clumsiest, most useless person I ever saw. It drives Stewart to chew nails sometimes! Wait until you see his paintings!" She laughed until tears came to her eyes.

"Not very good?" I asked, trying not to smile. I'd feared they'd be bad.

She shook her head. "Here's a nice sweater, dear. Garth gave it to me last Christmas."

I snuggled into it. "Thanks, Florence. I'd much rather wear one of your sweaters than one of Rosinna's."

"Don't be too hard on the poor woman. She tries hard. What she doesn't realize is that she doesn't have to be perfect to be a lady. She's full of fancy ideas though—her mother's ideas." We started back toward the kitchen. "I hope Jerome doesn't ask you to read one of his novels," she added. "His paintings will tickle you enough."

"Have you read any?"

"*All* of them, my dear. I feel like a well-paid and very patient mother to all these Glenden children. Yes, I've read every one of his works. We could use a few of them in the fireplace just now to warm things up a bit!"

I smothered another laugh.

"I mustn't do that," Florence scolded herself. "It's unkind. I'm afraid I've picked it up from Garth. He's a sarcastic rascal—also the most honest person I've ever known. All these manners and pretty talk Rosinna and Jerome value so much is just so much baloney to Garth. He attacks pretense every chance he gets."

"He doesn't lie?"

"Who, Garth? My goodness, he's as true as the day is long. You trust Garth, Merri, and you'll be in good hands."

We reached the stairs again. "I think I'll go see Stewart before I let Jerome show me his paintings."

"That'd be so nice of you, Merri. Stewart desperately needs loving attention."

"I'll say hello for you."

"Tell him I'll be up later to tidy his room. Maybe you can coax him out of it for a while. He'd do well with some fresh air. Poor man. The poor, poor man..." She went into the pantry, shaking her head.

I took the back stairs up just in case Rosinna or Jerome were waiting for me in the front. The house was utterly quiet, as if in a suspended hush. My pulse quickened as I hurried out of the morning room and down the hall.

Hesitating at Stewart's door, I tried to erase all worry from my face and put on a brave, believable smile. I knocked and waited, and knocked again when Stewart didn't answer. I didn't want to call out my name as I had the day before. Nothing was more painful than seeing his disappointment.

"Come in," he finally called softly. "Merri! I'm so glad to see you!"

He had dressed and shaved and again looked the picture of courage. He held out his hands and I took them, delighted he was feeling so well.

"You look much better today." I smiled. "Have I done you a little good?"

"More than you'll ever know," he said.

At once I realized he didn't smell of liquor. My face must have reflected my pleasure.

"That's right—no booze for breakfast. Is Florence still in the kitchen? I've been thinking of oatmeal. Would you join me?"

"I've already eaten, but I'll sit with you," I said, tugging at his hand.

Arm in arm we went down the staircase to the kitchen, commenting on the brilliant cobalt-blue sky and the chinook wind melting all the collected snow. When Florence saw us she threw up her hands and flew to Stewart.

"You look a hundred percent better!" she cried. "What can I fix for you, Mr. Glenden?"

"Some of your famous oatmeal—with apple and butter."

The slightest trace of shadow flickered across her eyes. "It's been months since I've made your favorite, Mr. Glenden. Please, sit down while I hunt up a fresh box."

I poured Stewart a cup of coffee.

"Have you and Garth made up yet?" Stewart asked, smiling at me.

I blushed. "I haven't talked to him yet."

"I did last night after you went to bed. I heard some of that tirade. I told Garth it was no way to treat a pretty young lady like you. You can take my word for it, he's very sorry, even without my prompting."

He latched onto his hot cup with a desperate grasp and sipped hurriedly. He needed a drink, but because of me, he was trying to put it off. I felt uneasy and guilty. I was doing just what I shouldn't, taking Merry's place in Stewart's mind. I would never be to him what she had been. Suddenly fearful, I felt myself withdraw from him. He had not burdened me before, but suddenly the weight of his happiness landed heavily on my shoulders. I worried I wasn't up to it.

Florence served the sweet, steaming oatmeal and Stewart tried valiantly to eat it. After a few swallows though, he paused. He pasted a new, more determined smile on his face and looked at me. "It's darn cold in here!"

"Garth's gone for a repairman," I said.

"I'm going back for a jacket," Stewart said, scraping up from the table abruptly. "Excuse me a moment, Merri. I'll be right back."

"Where's Mr. Glenden going?" Florence cried, seeing me alone at the table.

"For a jacket. He was cold."

Her mouth worked nervously. "The oatmeal," she whispered, "Right after Merry...left, he used to ask for it again and again. It broke him down after a while, remembering the bright mornings they'd spent together. It was something special between them because no one else liked it. Oh, it's silly of me to worry. I should be glad you've got him up."

We both burst into forced smiles as Stewart returned.

"It's not cold, is it? I hate cold oatmeal," he said, winking.

"Best hurry, Mr. Glenden," Florence said, edging back into the pantry.

"Would you like to see Jerome's gallery after breakfast?" I asked him. "They've offered to show me."

"Good grief, no!"

I caught the faint aroma of alcohol then and knew that he had gotten more than just his jacket when he went back to his room. Well, at least I wasn't a perfect substitute for Merry. I felt a sharp stab of disappointment nevertheless.

Managing to finish most of the oatmeal and coffee, Stewart finally suggested we see the library.

"Garth's told me a lot about it," I said, agreeing eagerly.

The vaulted room was opposite the dining room. It was a perfect library—dark and venerable, lined with books and dominated by a massive desk, chair and antique-gold globe. Stewart drew open the heavy red drapes. A blizzard of dust swirled through the brilliant rays of sunlight that slanted to the carpet. An especially blinding ray reflecting from the glaring ice outside hit a portrait standing on the desk. Inside the gold frame and brown oval mat was the photograph of a lovely young girl.

"Is that Natalie...or Merry?" I asked, deciding I might as well face whatever pain he must feel seeing it.

"It makes little difference," Stewart said. "They were so nearly the same. It used to bother me as Merry got older. I missed Natalie. We weren't together very many years—oh, the picture. It's Merry—her graduation picture. Gorgeous kid, isn't she?"

I nodded.

"I've got a feeling," Stewart said softly, after a thick pause. "I'm going to see her today."

My skin tightened and shivers ran along my spine. I didn't say anything because there was nothing *to* say after that. I just watched his face. There was such tenderness in his eyes. I felt embarrassed to watch. It was too intimate. I turned to a bank of books and let my eyes scan the titles sightlessly.

At last he cleared his throat and made a feeble attempt to laugh. "I used to work here." He sighed. "Now it's just a reminder of days when I was competent enough to manage Craggmoor's affairs. I leave that to Garth now, the real man of the house. Be patient with him, Merri. He's a good man, but he needs understanding and love. I'm glad you've come—not for myself so much, but for him. And, I guess Rosinna and Jerome too. I do care about them, though I've lost patience with them. I stay by myself because I know I make Rosinna feel helpless. Jerome knows I don't want him poking his nose into my life. You'd think *he* was my stepson, not Garth." He sighed again and shuffled to the door, suddenly looking exhausted.

I followed him out and reached for his hand. I steadied him as we went up the stairs. "Will you rest for a while?"

"Yes. That's a good idea."

"I mean really rest, Stewart. Don't stand by the window today. You need to lie down."

He shook his head firmly. "Today of all days I must be by the window. I'm going to see her. Merry is coming home today."

He walked slowly into his room and took up his place by the broad, sun-filled windows. He looked like a shadow against the brilliance. A painting flashed across my mind— deep gray around the edges, fading to a soft white in the middle. A dark, stooped figure stood in the middle outlined with a halo of brilliant white. I could almost feel the paint taking shape on a canvas. I wanted to capture forever the tragedy and beauty of a man's undying hope.

If I had been in a mood for jokes, the tour of the gallery would have been hilarious. I managed to keep a straight face somehow, but I don't mean from laughing. My throat ached with unexplained tears. Seeing Jerome's blundering efforts to make beauty out of paint annoyed me almost beyond endurance. I wanted to rip them up and take one of his unspoiled canvases and say, Here, look! This is what you should be painting, beauty, life, love; not drooping, dark, distorted things.

Jerome lectured me on every painting that hung in the room across the hall from his suite in the south wing. I had to sit on little velvet benches across from each one, so I could "fully appreciate" his genius. His paintings were ugly and dismal because he had overworked his colors and muddied them. How Rosinna could look on without betraying the truth, I didn't know.

I tried to be patient. I trailed after him, nodding and making polite little replies. The weight of boredom made me feel tired and heavy. Each time we moved to the next painting it was like making the supreme effort to lift each leg. My mind wandered and worried. I felt uneasy and listless. There was something important I should be doing, I thought, though I didn't know what. When Jerome pushed me into his studio to see his latest efforts, I could hardly manage to stay civil. Don't touch me with those clammy hands, I felt like snapping. Your paintings are dumb, dumb, dumb!

Rosinna went along like a doting mother appearing to think everything he did was fabulous. Finally—it seemed like hours—he ran out of canvases in progress. He turned for my final and best compliment.

"It was really great, Jerry." I smiled, trying desperately to sound sincere. "I sure wish I had the time to do so much."

"I'm sure you will, someday," he said, looking down his beak. "I'd be glad to help in any way I can. Maybe you'd like some lessons."

I almost choked.

"But you'd lose so much of your own valuable time," Rosinna put in.

"That's true." He sighed, considering what she had said. I was saved! For a moment I loved that green-eyed cat.

"I didn't realize how long it took to look at all your work," Rosinna said through a stifled yawn.

"I think I'll return Florence's sweater now," I said. I turned and went down the hall. "Thanks for the tour, Jerome."

"I'll see about lunch," Rosinna called after me.

I nodded and hurried away. Meals! I was tired of them. When out of their hearing, I sighed heavily. Lessons from Jerome! I was almost sick to my stomach!

Florence was nowhere around when I got to the kitchen. Something delicious simmered on the stove, and fresh-baked rolls cooled on the counter. I almost snitched one.

The gusting wind had died down. From the windows I could see some of the drive that went around back. The snow was melting in spots, but I saw no tracks. If Garth had left, wouldn't his car have left tire tracks in the snow?

I turned abruptly and ran up the back stairs, being careful to avoid the ripped carpet on the top step. The ghostly morning room was bitter cold. The hall wasn't so bad by then. When I got to Garth's room and knocked, no one answered.

I peeked in. His bed was unmade. Shoes and socks lay scattered on the floor. A briefcase lay opened on the bed. If Garth wasn't in his room or in the furnace room and hadn't driven away, where else could he be?

I tiptoed down the back stairs. My blood raced and made me dizzy. I really didn't know what I was doing. It was hard enough to think. I kept racing from one question to another. Did he go out the front way? Was there another driveway? Had he gone at all?

Florence was back in the pantry. I could hear her beating something in a bowl. Rosinna's crisp voice came from not far away. "She *did* like them, Jerome," she insisted quietly. "I'm sure she did." Teacups clinked.

"She assumes she's better than I," Jerome muttered peevishly.

"Where would you get such an idea? Merri was very polite and showed interest in all your paintings. She can hardly know more about art than you. She's not even graduated from a reputable school."

"I don't care for her," he said.

I curbed my urge to add my own opinions—mentally.

"When is she leaving?" I heard him ask.

"We can't be rude. Garth and Stewart want her to stay."

I edged closer to the doorway. Florence appeared from the pantry, but her back was to me so she didn't see me standing there. She put her hands on her hips and huffed. "Lunch is served."

As she disappeared into the pantry, I slipped around the corner and stopped on the top step of the stairs leading to the tunnel. I held my breath. I wasn't really sure if they could see me from where they sat. I didn't even know what I intended to do. I just knew I didn't want to be seen.

When Rosinna and Jerome came into the kitchen and pulled out their chairs, I hurried down to the tunnel.

It was dark. Half the overhead bulbs were out. I wasn't sure which door led to the furnace room. Garth had pointed it out, but I couldn't remember.

The tunnel was about eight feet wide. As far as I could estimate, it went on for about fifty yards before it reached the door to the garage.

Doors were spaced every fifteen feet. I peeked into the first one. The wine racks looked dusty and murky in the dim light filtering through the iron-barred window near the ceiling.

I switched on the light. No one was in there.

My heart thudded as I hurried to the next door and

looked in. The larder was a large room with shelves upon shelves of boxed and canned goods. Across from me stood two upright freezers humming quietly.

Across the hall I found the furnace room. I switched on the light and went in. No one was there, either. The body of the huge gray furnace loomed in the middle of the room like some sleeping monster. My eyes followed the many arms of the octopus-like air ducts snaking across the ceiling and disappearing into the walls.

Next to me the door to the fuse box hung open. Garth's brown jacket was draped over it! I grabbed the sleeve and held it for a moment. The fabric was warm and scratchy in my hand. I couldn't see Garth going out in that wind without it.

All right, I told myself. Stay calm. He's still in the house somewhere. Maybe he's sulking because he can't fix the furnace.

I plunged my hand into the first pocket I found. His car keys were in it—and two screws. I looked at them for a moment. Screws. I held them up. The gray paint on the heads just matched the door of the panel from the furnace that lay upside down on the floor. I peeked into the furnace at the long rows of burners deep inside. It was as ancient as the old cookstove in Aunt Coral's garage. I stuck my head in farther. There was no flame where I guessed the pilot light should be.

Maybe Garth went into the tool room. Of course! He couldn't do a thing without a hammer or wrench. I turned off the light and plunged myself into utter darkness. It was awful in there—but I forced myself to listen for sounds out in the tunnel. Nothing.

Relieved, I got out of the menacing darkness and hurried to the next door, hoping it was the tool room. It opened a crack and then bumped against something heavy. I pushed as hard as I could. It gave a little. Maybe if I threw my weight against it...

Something made a grunt!

My heart leaped with alarm. I jerked back.

A hand—a bloody hand—closed around the lower edge of the door and then fell limp!

A scream rose in my throat. I choked it back and crouched, convulsing with fear and revulsion. I pushed on the door a little more, feeling a shudder crawl up my back.

I heard another moan.

My hair stood on end. "Garth? Is that you?"

"Merri?"

Again his bloody hand seized the door. It opened enough for me to squeeze through. Once in I hit the light and bent over Garth's body. I slipped to the floor and took his head in my arms.

Six

"Let me go for help!" I said.

Garth slumped against me on the floor of the tool room. He winced when I smoothed back his hair. There was a terrible lump on the back of his head. The cut had stopped bleeding, but it was badly swollen.

"No, Merri, wait." He tried to ease up on one elbow. "I'll be all right."

"How long have you been in here?"

"I don't know. A long time."

"Florence said you came down to fix the furnace. That was before breakfast! What happened?"

"I came in here to get...tools. The furnace was turned off."

My stomach began to feel queasy. Who would have done such a thing?

"I came down to breakfast...I wanted to tear into Rosinna for turning off the heat again..." He eased upright and patted his head gingerly. "Oh! That hurts. Rosinna said the thermostat wasn't working—or some fool thing." Garth shook his head slowly. "The wires were disconnected. I think it was a setup. Somebody was waiting for me."

"And hit you?" I cried.

"Did a good job of it, too. I've been half conscious. I got to the door, but passed out."

"I was just down here an hour or so ago!" I said, smoothing back his blood-crusted hair. "Here, let me help you up. You're a mess."

He laughed through his teeth. "Stop crying, Merri. I'll be okay as soon as I get something cold on my head and something hot in my veins." He reached up and pushed the tears off my cheeks. His eyes looked soft.

"They said you'd left." I grunted under the weight of his arm as we both struggled to our feet.

"Yeah? Likely story."

"Jerome said you drove the maid into town."

"She left last night." Garth winced as he spoke. Then he grinned. "Were you just a little jealous, I hope?"

"Rosinna said you just gave up and went home." I ignored his tease. He might want to pass this off lightly, but I didn't.

"Ah, a handy explanation for every mysterious event," he said taking a step. He swayed dangerously. "Give me your hand. I'm still seeing double."

"You'd better see a doctor. Something could be broken."

"Not this head—too thick. Hurry up. I don't want anyone to see me just yet. Whoever did it isn't much of a villain. Leaving bodies around is sloppy."

"Do you suppose Rosinna or Jerome did it?"

"I did at first." Then he shook his head. "I think your

mysterious prowler did it. Who would have the guts to knock me over the head? Jerry? That dope couldn't step on a bug."

"We have to do something about your head!" I said as I studied him.

"Yeah, have it examined."

"Let me get you some coffee."

"No, no. Let's get out of here. We'll go to my apartment. I'll come back later and tear Craggmoor apart with my bare hands."

"If you think I'd let you come back here with some nut out for your scalp…"

"Why, Merri! Do I detect a note of concern?"

"Stop teasing. I'm not going anywhere. We'll go right up and find out who did this to you."

"Do you know what we might be getting into?" he demanded, grabbing me with rubbery fingers.

"You're in no shape to do anything. You can't even squeeze my arm. Please, Garth. Let me help you."

He shook his head and staggered. "Somebody's hiding something pretty big. Why else would they be so desperate to stop us from asking questions? I don't want you mixed up in it," Garth said.

"I'm not leaving you!"

He hugged me weakly. "See if the tunnel is deserted. We'll go to Florence's room and get something for my headache. Will they miss you a few minutes more?"

My pulse quickened. "I should be there right now. They're having lunch."

"Just great." He sighed. "They'll come looking for you pretty soon. If we leave now we won't have to face them until we've decided what to do."

I shook my head.

"I don't understand."

I made him pause long enough to look at me. "I'm sorry about last night," I said. "You were absolutely right about me. Yesterday I wanted to run from all this. I'm mixed up in it now, whether you like it or not. I want to find out what's going on."

"You're hopeless."

I nodded with a smile. After I peeked into the tunnel and saw nothing, Garth and I ran to Florence's room and found a bandage for his head. He complained just like a little kid when I put it on. He didn't look nearly so bad once I got him cleaned up.

"I'm going out to the garage," he said over a mouthful of water and aspirin. "You have lunch and act as if nothing's wrong. Don't tell them you found me. I know you don't want to play spy, but anything Rosinna or Jerry say could be a clue. So help me, if one of them brained me—I'm not a lawyer for nothing."

"It won't work," I sighed.

"You can't do it?"

"I can't sit there eating creamed chicken while you're in danger."

"I'll be safe in my car. After that we're getting out of here."

"I just got done telling you I don't want to go. What can we find out if we leave?"

"We have to have some kind of plan. I don't like to think about what comes after a skull fracture. Please, Merri. I don't want to risk our lives!"

His hands on my shoulders melted my determination.

Maybe we should go. I couldn't stand it if anything happened to him.

"We'll have a head start if you go up and have lunch and then tell me everything. You can do it," he said.

"Maybe I could get Rosinna to give herself away," I said hopefully.

Garth's eyes glinted. He was trying to trick me, I realized. He wanted to confuse me so I'd leave with him. He was lying and I saw right through it. He intended to handle Rosinna and Jerome alone while I sat helplessly at his apartment.

Garth could hardly see straight. He kept touching his forehead and wincing. Every time he saw me notice it he shrugged it off.

"I won't try anything alone," he said. "If I call the police after we get down to the Springs, would that make you feel better?"

"It sure would!"

"We can't call them from here."

"You're right," I said, letting my face fall and pretending to be convinced. So that was his plan.

I had to trick him into leaving. I knew my prowler didn't intend to hurt me. Garth was the one in danger. If anyone had to get to safety, it was he.

"I see wheels turning in your pretty head that I don't like," Garth grumbled.

"I've been gone so long. What'll I tell them?"

"That's my girl! You'll know what to say. But hurry. The red car parked on this end of the garage is mine. Get lunch over with and then get down here. We'll be able to call the cops long before those two hyenas suspect we're onto them."

"I bet we find Merry by tonight, too." I smiled. "Maybe

she thought no one wanted her to come back. Ever think of that? I'll meet you at the car in fifteen minutes."

"Stay cool. If anything goes wrong..." He looked uneasy.

"Nothing will," I reassured him, touching his arm gently. "This isn't a matter of life and death, you know."

"I hope not," he said, touching his sore head skeptically. "I sure hope not."

He edged past me, squinting to see. Suddenly he stopped, turned and looked down at me. "Did I tell you I've fallen in love with you?"

For a moment I couldn't breathe. My heart shivered with excitement. He loved me—this handsome, smart, lovable guy loved me. I wanted to throw my arms around his neck. I wanted to tell him something crazy had happened inside my heart in the past forty-eight hours too. But if I said a single word of it, neither of us would ever get to the secret of what happened to Merry.

I kept my arms firmly at my sides. His lips touched mine. I felt myself weaken. Go with him, I kept thinking. Go away from this place. He loves me. What else matters? Even yet, I didn't move. He had to go—for his own safety—his life!

Finally he pulled away, smiling uncertainly. "Don't be long. I don't want to lose you too."

I shook my head and watched him trot awkwardly down the tunnel past the burned-out bulbs to the door leading to the garage.

"Garth, wait," I called. The words came before I could stop them. No, I had to let him go. I had to. That wasn't red paint on his shirt. Someone wanted to kill Garth! "Your coat!" I dashed into the furnace room to get it and ran after him. "It's...cold."

I put it across his broad shoulders. When I reached to pat him, he was already through the door. I missed.

Florence had just finished the lunch dishes. "Why, Merri! I've been worried. Where've you been?"

"Returning your sweater." I tried to smile innocently.

She frowned. I caught her looking at me out of the corner of her eye.

"Did I miss lunch?" I asked.

"There's a bit left. I was about to bring it up to you."

"Well, there you are," Rosinna called from behind. "I was just up in your room looking for you. Florence said you were resting."

"You must have just missed me," I said, accepting a plate from Florence. "I came down the back stairs." I couldn't look at Florence, but I looked Rosinna right in the eye.

"They are handy, aren't they?" Rosinna smiled. "I'll have more tea, thank you, Florence. I'll keep Merri company while she eats. You've been resting a lot. I hope you're not ill."

"I don't think so. Maybe it's the altitude."

I forced myself to eat slowly. "Jerome's paintings were interesting," I said rather lamely.

"He's dedicated to his work. I don't know which he prefers, painting or writing. He goes at both with such passion."

"Discussing me?" Jerome asked, coming in from the den. "I have a fire going now. Come in where it's warm."

I picked up my plate and followed Rosinna and Jerome into the den. When I finished eating, Florence took my plate, bending low to give me a stern look.

The time dragged. Jerome chattered about his work, occasionally giving me odd looks. He wanted me to praise his paintings, so I showed the most sincere interest I could. I asked him about technique and color and canvas. I thought I was doing very well.

Rosinna became bored. Her back almost sagged as she sat staring into the fire.

"I wish Garth would hurry with that repairman," I said suddenly. My face burned treacherously.

"A repairman?" Jerome said, turning, his icy eyes boring through me.

"Florence said he went to get one. It felt warmer a minute ago, but now I'm cold again."

Jerome sniffed. "He's probably stuck in a snow drift again."

Rosinna didn't jump to add her criticism. "If you'll excuse me," she added abruptly.

"What's wrong?" Jerome demanded.

"I don't feel well. I'm going to my room." She gave me an apologetic look and hurried out.

"Forgive Rosinna. I've tired her with all my talk," Jerome said. "She so admires talent and has so little herself. I'm afraid I've made her feel badly."

I looked around the room trying not to agree or disagree. Finally he moved toward the door, his shoes whisper-quiet on the carpet. "I'll check on her and then I have some work to do."

"Don't mind me." I smiled, relieved.

He excused himself and went through the kitchen to the main hall. I hopped up right after him and listened. I hardly heard him go up the staircase.

When all was quiet I nearly flew down the stairs to the tunnel. Only pausing a moment to check my way clear, I rushed down the tunnel and threw open the door to the garage.

Garth had the garage door up. It was bitter cold. The car's motor was running. I closed the door from the tunnel behind me and called.

He sat up fast and grabbed at his head. "Ugh! You sure took your time."

"Garth, I can't go yet."

His face folded into an angry frown. "What's wrong now?"

"I...I can't leave Stewart. Wait till I get him."

"Get in this car right now before I get mad!"

I waved my arm frantically. "Sh-h-h!"

"I will not. What's gotten into you?"

"I'm not going! Now get out of here before I tell Rosinna and Jerome."

"My God, Merri! Have you gone crazy? You can't tell them anything they don't already know."

When he climbed from the car, I shook my head and rushed back to the door. He looked so terribly hurt and angry. I couldn't stand it.

"I'm not leaving here until you get in that car," he yelled. "I'm warning you."

"No!" I tried to look confident. "You're trying to trick me!"

"You're in danger here!"

"You don't think I believed that, do you? I've known all along it was you." I tore open the door and slammed it behind me. Just as Garth reached it, I threw the bolt closed.

"I can't believe this!" he shouted through the door.

I ran. I had done it! As long as he was locked out, he was safe. Now I could march right up to Rosinna's room and...

I was just passing the darkest stretch in the tunnel. A door opened beside me. I whirled. A shadowy figure grabbed me and cut off my scream. I struggled and for a moment felt myself overcoming the hold around my chest. Then suddenly I was thrust into darkness. I fell and hit my head against a wall and lay helpless.

It had to be a man! It had to be, I told myself. Just from the way he breathed and grunted. I began to sit up and shook my head so I could get a clear look at him. My eyes had just about adjusted to the darkness when something—a piece of cloth tasting oily and dusty—pressed against my mouth. It was the wrong time to scream. The rag went in my mouth and was tied fast. He jerked one of my arms behind my back and began to wind a rope tighter and tighter...

Suddenly he stopped, as if listening. I didn't hear anything. He let out a disagreeable grunt of fear and bolted from the room. The door slammed shut and I was lost in the darkness.

For several minutes I lay still, numbed by surprise and fear. Who would dare...The gag's nasty taste made my stomach lurch. When I finally realized I *could* move and rolled over, I got a deep breath and just about passed out.

Now I'd done it. Me and my big ideas. Find out the secret without Garth's help—I could have laughed if I hadn't already been crying. Where was I and how was I going to get out?

It was almost too easy to get free. I struggled to sit up. The rope was more tangled around my wrists than tied. I loosened the gag and spat it out. Just when I could get a good breath for scream, a huge roar went up beside me. I smelled gas! I nearly climbed the wall trying to get out of the way. My feet hit something and I went flying. I hit hard and didn't have enough breath left in my lungs to say a prayer!

With a blinding flash, the flames swept across the gas burners in the lower regions of the furnace. The tremendous blower began forcing warm air up through the ducts. It sounded like the inside of an old-time locomotive.

The room filled with an eerie blue light. It was no use. My screams were too faint. I sat up rubbing my head and sniffling. What next?

Across the room, a row of cabinets stood under a dim, barred window. It looked as if, could I climb them, I might be able to get out, or at least see out and call for help.

The cabinets were old and wobbly. I braced my foot on the door handle and eased up to the gritty, dusty top. Through the window I could see the curve of the driveway behind Craggmoor.

Garth's car stood there idling.

"Garth!" I screamed. "Don't go!"

He came into my line of view, pacing angrily. He smoked in huge gulps and then threw down the butt, grinding it into the drive and casting contemptuous looks back toward the garage.

Don't give up, I prayed. Come back for me. Don't go! I need help. Try to get back in. Surely you know a way…

He got in the car. I burst out crying. "Don't leave me!" I shouted until my voice turned to a whisper. "Oh, God, don't leave me!"

But, at last, he spun the tires and inched up the hill until he disappeared onto the highway.

How could he go? How could he really go? I wept. I stared at the spot where he'd disappeared, hoping he'd come back. My fingers got tired gripping the windowsill. My arms began to shake. Standing on top of the cabinet in pitch darkness wasn't exactly steady. I turned awkwardly to get down. The cabinet began to tip. I jumped. My legs and feet stung so much when I hit the floor that I crashed against the furnace. Behind me, one of the cabinets fell. I leaped out of the way, feeling like the whole room was collapsing around me.

By then, I was so rattled that I had to sit and let my head clear. I felt along the walls back to the door. The light switch wouldn't work. I sank to the floor.

The furnace rumbled. It seemed to suck the moisture from the air. Soon my tongue and lips and eyes burned from the heat. I couldn't think. I felt woozy in the gassy darkness. Open the window, I thought. At least get some fresh air.

The fallen cabinet was heavy. I tried lifting it, but the doors kept falling open and hitting me in the shins. Filters, tools, and fuses clattered around my feet. Here was what Garth had needed all along to fix the stupid furnace, I thought, as something big hit my leg and fell to the floor.

It was no use. I couldn't get it back up. I kicked everything out of my way. The big thing bumped me again and I reached for it.

It was a suitcase.

A suitcase in a cabinet in the furnace room? I crouched down and tried to undo the latches. My fingers began to tremble. I tried not to think.

One latch flipped open. I struggled over the other. It

stuck. I hit it, growing more and more uneasy. A suitcase—a suitcase? The latch gave at last. When I lifted the top, dresses fell out.

I sank to the floor. What did it mean? Four dresses—that was all. No underwear, no shoes, no nothing. Four dresses missing from the very center of Merry's closet. Four dresses and a suitcase and...Merry.

My heart felt leaden and tired. I sighed heavily and tried for a moment not to think at all. A suitcase...Garth was hit over the head. I was trapped. The suitcase she supposedly took was still here. What did it all mean?

Either Merry never left Craggmoor, or she was dead and someone hid her suitcase to cover the evidence. Maybe she was prisoner somewhere, I thought hopefully. Craggmoor was so big...Rosinna shut Stewart in his room when he was drunk. She could just as easily have kept Merry locked up to keep her from that "unsuitable" man.

For two years? I asked myself. I pushed the suitcase off my lap and got up. I had to stop kidding myself. This was no cat-and-mouse game. Somebody meant business and was playing for keeps.

I had to get out. If I yelled loud enough or pounded the door hard enough, wouldn't Florence hear me? I felt along the wall to the door and started in, first with my fists, then my feet, then my fists again.

I tired quickly. "Florence? Let me out!" I screamed. My throat burned. My hands began to ache.

No answer came. What if she didn't come down all day—what if they did something to Florence too, like they had to Garth and me? She might never come down and hear me calling. I could die there, I thought. I could die!

I felt dizzy. Oh, Garth, come back for me, I cried. Let me out!

I beat the door harder and harder. "Can't anyone hear me?" In desperation I threw myself against the door and then slid down to the floor. No use, no use.

Suddenly the furnace stopped roaring. The blower went off. The gas jets winked out. The room went completely dark except for the tiny blue pilot light deep inside. Who lit that? I wondered. Then it was so utterly quiet, it was creepy. My skin began to crawl.

Take it easy, I told myself. Everything's going to be all right now. "Florence!" I called in a more normal, but hoarse, voice. "I'm locked in the furnace room."

My words echoed down the tunnel. When I heard them bounce around inside the quiet furnace I got an idea. My voice might carry upstairs through the air ducts!

"Stewart!" I yelled into the furnace. "I'm downstairs—locked in the furnace room. Let me out!"

I repeated that more slowly, listening to my eerie echo pass upward. I shuddered. Please be sober enough to understand, I thought. "Stewart! It's Merri. I need help! Help!"

Then out in the tunnel I heard running.

Garth was back! I thought. "Help me! I'm in here!" I yelled, flinging an aching palm against the door.

The footsteps stopped.

"Let me out!" I started pounding again. When I stopped to listen, it seemed too quiet. Who was out there?

Suddenly terrified, I couldn't make another sound. Every click and hiss inside the cooling furnace ripped my nerves until I was ready to scream. Who was out there? Was it time to finish me off?

I jumped when the footsteps pounded back down the tunnel. "Don't go!"

I screamed until I was too hoarse to make another sound. Why wouldn't anyone help me? I fell to the floor exhausted. I would never get out. I was trapped. A strange calm settled over me. It was like being dead. I was going to lie there forever. I couldn't imagine *ever* finding a way out. I couldn't imagine anything—just darkness. The room cooled. Whiffs of fresh air sneaked under the door. I turned my head to it and sniffed. The light under the door was a vague comfort. If I stayed quiet...

I thought I heard someone calling. I thought of Aunt Coral, of the fire, my plane trip to Colorado, Garth, the cold forbidding face of Craggmoor and its stone wall—

"Mer-r-ry!" came the faint cry. "I'm coming!"

I managed to get up on one elbow.

"Merry! Merry!"

For a long moment everything was absolutely quiet. Not a creak or footstep or whisper of wind penetrated my prison. Then came an awful scream. My whole body convulsed when I heard it. I covered my ears to escape the sound of it piercing my head. Someone screamed again and again. I edged closer to the crack under the door. My forehead bumped it and colored stars went off behind my eyes. Oh please, I wept, enough!

The doorknob rattled. I was on my feet in a split second. I wrenched the doorknob and it turned! The lighted tunnel nearly blinded me!

Blinking back tears of joy, I threw the door open and fell into the tunnel. How good the light was! How cool and fresh the air! I stumbled toward the stairs laughing and crying. "I'm out!"

"What happened?" Florence was waiting in the front hall when I burst into the kitchen. I plunged through the door. Rosinna and Florence were crouched on the floor beside a body.

"Merri!" Rosinna shrieked, standing up. "He fell! He fell all the way down the stairs and he hasn't moved!"

I took one last step and froze. Stewart lay sprawled at their feet. No! I thought. He was just…No! No! I began to shake my head. The skin across my forehead felt tight. My hair was prickling all over my head and for a horrid moment I thought I was going to be sick.

Jerome plunged about halfway down the staircase and then stopped, clutching the thick banister with thin, white hands. He stared down at us, his eyes bulging, his mouth stretched into something ugly. He took another uncertain step and let out a childlike cry. Florence twisted her dish towel around her fingers as she stared at me. Then abruptly she jerked her head away.

Rosinna flung herself at me and sobbed on my shoulder. I pushed her away. Stewart lay face down, one arm thrown out to his side, his thin legs tangled underneath him. He didn't move, or breathe, or make the slightest sound. I stepped closer, bent, and touched his tousled hair. This time I recognized death instantly.

Then I fell on him, crying, trying to gather him into my arms. "Don't be dead!"

He was a lifeless rag doll in my arms. I felt a pain so deep in my heart that I feared for a moment I might die too. It wasn't so! It didn't happen! It couldn't—not again!

Florence pried me free. I fell against her, sobbing,

pulling at her strong, comforting arms in an effort to shake loose the grief.

Jerome slipped down the remaining steps and went to Rosinna, taking her gently in his arms. He wept too—we all did. Tragedy again had struck Craggmoor. But only I, and one other person among us, knew just how tragic this senseless accident really was.

"What happened?" I whispered, suddenly able to pull away from Florence and look down at the man I'd pretended was my new father.

The four of us faced each other. Rosinna kept her eyes averted from Stewart's body. Tears dripped from her chin. Jerome looked ashen and wobbly. I don't think he really knew what was going on. Florence sniffed and dabbed her eyes with her dish towel.

"It was the strangest thing," Rosinna whimpered. "I was in my room and I heard a voice very far away. It sounded just like Merry! She called Stewart again and again. Oh, it was awful! For a moment, I thought I had lost my mind. Stewart must have heard it too because suddenly his door crashed open. He ran down the hall calling her. Before I could catch up to him..." She burst into fresh tears and fell against Jerome.

"I heard it, too," Florence said with amazement. "Mr. Glenden tore out of his room. I heard him give a cry at the top of the stairs. And then the awful fall, tumbling over and over again to the very bottom."

"Florence, please," Rosinna moaned.

"Oh, my Lord! I wish Garth were here," Florence went on, not even hearing Rosinna.

I was speechless. My calls for help had brought Stewart

to his death!

Florence steadied me. We all made it to the den somehow. I sat stiffly in the chair. Rosinna fell onto the couch and sobbed. Jerome looked confused. He started in one direction and stopped, turning another way. His face was slack and he kept blinking, like he was trying to think.

"Hadn't you better call the doctor—and the police?" Florence said.

A wind had started up again outside. It whispered against the windows, making me shiver. Finally Jerome reached for the phone.

Stewart had been expecting to see Merry all day, I thought miserably. His last thought had been of her. Why hadn't I realized how it would have sounded to him?

And yet...Stewart would never have to know what I found in the furnace room. I was almost glad he was dead. I don't know how I would have told him Merry never left Craggmoor. Maybe it had been an accident, Merry's mysterious disappearance. She could have simply fallen into the lake, or something like that. But the suitcase...

I had to get away from Jerome and Rosinna and...the horror. I went up the back stairs to my room. Everything would be all right when Garth got back, I thought. He would know what to do. I locked my door and washed my smudged face and brushed the dust and cobwebs from my hair. Then I lay down. My mind spun. My heart wouldn't stop racing. Stewart was dead. No, I couldn't let myself think about that because if I did I'd blame myself, just like I had when Aunt Coral died. I couldn't take it, not a second time. No, I didn't dare think of it.

The suitcase—I kept seeing the suitcase; Garth's bloody

hand, his angry face; the dark, stuffy furnace room; Stewart at the bottom of the stairs…Garth's bloody hand…

Those horrible, fragmented thoughts were still galloping through my head when someone banged the doorknocker an hour later. I sat up too fast—Garth?

The knock came again before Jerome and Rosinna answered it. "My father," Jerome said bluntly. "He had an accident."

It was the police and ambulance. At the top of the stairs I watched orderlies lift Stewart onto a stretcher, cover him, and wheel him out. Two policemen remained in the entrance hall, talking to Jerome and Rosinna, watching me as I came down the stairs.

"He'd been drinking?" one of them was asking.

Rosinna nodded, reluctantly, dabbing at her swollen eyes. "He's had a…drinking problem for years, you see. He was coming down the stairs when he lost his balance."

"And where were you, Miss Glenden?" he asked her.

"In my room."

"May I present our cousin Merri Glenden from Illinois," Jerome said stiffly. "She's visiting.

"I'm so glad you were here to make Stewart's last days happier," Rosinna cried unexpectedly and with so much sincerity that I actually believed her.

The policeman nodded to me. "Miss Glenden was in her room. Mr. Glenden was also. The cook was cleaning up in the kitchen."

Florence nodded solemnly from the shadows.

"And you, miss? Where were you?"

Rosinna and Jerome looked at me. One of them had locked me in that room. I took a deep breath. "I was returning the sweater I borrowed from Florence. I was downstairs when I heard all the noise."

"What noise?" the policeman asked, making me feel like they were closing in on me.

I shrank from them. "Rosinna's scream. When I came up they were all here crying because…because…" I turned away and gulped back tears. "He may have drunk too much, but we all loved him just the same!"

After a few more questions, the policemen left. Florence turned away, visibly tired and shaky. Jerome started up the staircase. "I think I'll go…rest."

Rosinna wrung her hands. "I should make arrangements." She pushed at her hair and messed it up. Then she started up the stairs too and paused. "I'm…so confused." She went on, muttering something about not having a suitable black dress to wear.

For the life of me I didn't know if either of them realized I'd lied or not. I had to talk to someone. The world was flying apart around me. I started after Florence, deciding to tell her everything. She'd help. I raced down the stairs after her.

When I stepped into the tunnel everything went dark. I squawked. A huge hand clapped across my mouth. It was the same hand, the same trembling, vicelike grip that had held me fast a few eternal nights ago!

I struggled, but it was useless. I had had too much happen in too short a time, and at last I fell into a merciful fog of unconsciousness.

Seven

Something wet touched my forehead. I opened my eyes. A man was bending over me—a man I had never seen before. I shrank from him, biting hard to keep from yelling. I looked around and found myself in a small, rustic living room, not in the tunnel where I had fainted. "Where..."

He offered me a steaming cup of coffee. "I'm not going to hurt you." He talked to me as if I were a frightened and cornered animal. "I'm sorry I scared you. I didn't mean to. Try to understand." He had large, soft eyes that reminded me of a deer. He urged the coffee cup into my hand. The way he gripped it made me think he was more afraid of me than I was of him. "Please, have some coffee."

I sat up and took the cup. The room was chilly, sparsely furnished. It looked like no one had lived there in a while. Seeing me looking around, he explained. "This is the gardener's house. It's over the garage. I'm the ex-gardener, Tom McPhee."

I clapped my hand over my mouth. So! I had been right

all along! There *was* another man at Craggmoor, a strong man, by the look of his thick arms. "Weren't you fired?" I asked, getting confused.

"Practically arrested," he barked, standing up and moving around like he was caged. Just as quickly he masked his anger, smiled, and shook his shoulders. "I'm sorry. You wouldn't know what I've been through all this time—not knowing, half fearing—I heard you calling a while ago. I phoned Garth, but he wasn't at his office or home."

"How did you…"

"We knew each other when I worked here. He's the only decent one in the family. You know, when I saw the ambulance pull up, I thought they'd finally done you in. What's happened?"

"Stewart fell down the stairs." I had to stop when my throat closed. I blinked and kept my eyes averted for a minute.

"Is he hurt?"

"He's…dead."

Tom didn't speak for several minutes. He stared out a window and finally, when I'd gotten myself in control, he turned. "I swear, there's something hidious about this place. I was so close to getting Merry away—so close! But Rosinna wrecked it." He clenched his fists. "I'm a nice ordinary guy, a guy who likes to plant flowers and tend trees. Those no-good Glendens. Look what they've turned me into—a criminal. You didn't know I was hanging around watching everyone, did you?" He paused and thought a minute. "Or maybe you did. I'm sorry. I can tell by the look of you that you don't know why I'm here. I was Merry's husband."

I couldn't help look surprised.

"We were married for four lousy hours before they got their hooks into her and packed her off someplace. Whether Merry still wants me or not, I mean to find out where she is. I'll do anything."

"Rosinna mentioned…Merry was involved with someone." I didn't know how to put it politely. "I thought she was lying!"

"I wasn't good enough." He snorted. "I loved Merry—I loved her! I would have made her happy. But a Glenden," he said with curled lips, "couldn't possibly move into the gardener's house. And the gardener certainly couldn't live in Craggmoor." He made a disgusted noise. "That old girl's got a way with words, doesn't she?"

"Rosinna said that?"

"The day she fired me."

"Then she knew about you. Merry told her." I couldn't make sense of it. If Rosinna knew Merry wanted to marry the gardener, then surely she did know where Merry was!

"If I'd had any brains I'd never have brought Merry back here. I should have taken her away when I had the chance. But no—she wanted to tell Stewart. She wanted him to give her away. I'd talked her out of that. If we were already married by the time she told everyone, Rosinna couldn't do anything to stop it—or so I thought."

"Rosinna knew you were already married? You're sure?" None of it made any sense.

"Sure, she did. I swear, I'll kill that woman. Two years! Two years I've waited. I've written every college and private school in the country. Merry must be in Europe."

"I'm mixed up." I set the empty coffee cup down. Rosinna had claimed all this time that nothing unusual had happened the day Merry disappeared.

"I'll get more coffee and start from the beginning."

I watched him slop coffee all over the counter in the kitchen. He muttered under his breath and finally gave up trying to clean up after himself.

He came back and sat across from me. The coffee stung his lips. He pressed them together and sighed raggedly. "You think I'm crazy, but I've been driven to do a lot of rotten things since Merry went away. I spend hours on a road five miles out where I can see up here with my binoculars. I follow Rosinna when I get the chance—which isn't often. She hibernates up here—but the other day I spotted her leaving, caught up to her and followed her. She went to the post office." He sipped loudly. "Who are you, anyway?"

"My name is Merri, too." I told him how I came to Craggmoor.

"I saw Rosinna mail that letter. I thought…"

"How did you get onto the grounds?" I asked.

"When Rosinna ran me off two years ago I disconnected the alarm across the back. I come and go as I want—anyone could. I couldn't care less. Somebody could steal the silver spoons right from their mouths and I'd just stand there. Maybe I'd even lend a hand." He tried to laugh that off, but his eyes betrayed his sincerity. "Merry was a great girl— pretty, always laughing, honest. I was crazy about her."

"How did you meet her?"

"I started working here five years ago. I liked the pay but not the Royal Pair. During the summer Merry used to help me decide where to plant new lilacs and rosebushes. I grew some special American Beauties that she liked to put on her mother's grave down in the Springs."

"Then you didn't know Natalie."

He shook his head. "Merry and Garth missed her a lot. Garth was just back from Harvard then—cocky as the devil. We got along, but he was hostile, you know? He had a chip on his shoulder the size of a railroad tie."

"I know."

"Merry was just a kid. We'd work in the garden. That drove Rosinna nuts. I helped Merry grow pumpkins for Halloween that first year. She got a bang out of that. Rosinna was a tyrant, made Merry behave proper. With Garth working so much and only the Royal Pair to talk to, she got lonely. I was handy at first, I guess. Later on, she loved me as much as I loved her—at least I thought so then. I hope Rosinna didn't change that."

"Rosinna told me Merry ran away to get married," I said. "How did she make it sound so much like a lie?"

"Because she didn't *run* away at all. She was sent away from lowborn me. She's probably a prisoner in some rotten girl's school in Switzerland."

"Rosinna told Garth Merry ran away from the money."

"Garth didn't swallow that, did he?"

"No."

"Rosinna know's exactly what she's doing," Tom snarled.

"Garth's still got a detective looking for her."

"A lot of good that's done. He ought to just make Rosinna tell."

"How could you wait all this time?"

"What else could I do? They've got money and power. When you're dealing with people like the Glendens, you don't do anything straightforward. You should hear some of the things I've heard Rosinna and Jerome talk about when they're alone. They were ready to have you arrested. I overheard you, too, a couple of times. What was that all about with Garth earlier? I almost let him back in when you locked him out. Then things started happening…He didn't grab you. It was me—me out on your balcony—me in the morning room."

I glared at him. "Was it you who hit Garth over the head this morning? Somebody was out to get him. I figured if he left he might live a little longer." When Tom stared at me in amazement, I shrugged. "Well, it made sense at the time."

"It wasn't me," Tom said. "Garth treated me like a friend."

"Then what were you doing on my balcony?"

"I saw you coming up the drive that day. I thought Merry was coming back—I'd been hanging around a couple of days. Anyway, I figured I could help her get away after dark and hide, just in case Rosinna made a search. How was I to know they'd give you the room I was hiding in? Every time I tried to get out the maid would come in. I'm sorry, but I got cold! I thought Rosinna followed me into the morning room, not you. By then I was so miserable—Merry wasn't back after all—I just grabbed. The next morning Rosinna came up while I was listening. It was all I could do to get away. Rosinna's probably known all along it was me in the house. I told her I'd be back someday."

"Some of the things that have happened make sense now," I said. "Did Rosinna have reason to hate you, or was she just being a snob?"

"It would have made Rosinna happy if Merry turned out to be an old cow just like her. Yeah, I guess she had reason. I never meant to get serious, though. I was honorable as hell—knew my place, as Rosinna said so often. Merry used to come to me at night before Stewart stopped drinking. She and I would sit up here for hours talking. I'd hold her and listen to her cry. I loved her—I couldn't help myself. Stewart put her and the whole family through hell, but they went on loving him. Merry did everything she could think of to get him to quit drinking. It wasn't until he nearly died that he finally realized he had to change. Merry needed me most then. She'd come here after twenty-four or thirty-six hours at the hospital. It tore me up to see her cry like she did. I'm only human. I fell in love and I wanted to get her away from Craggmoor."

"When did you get married?"

"At first we planned to wait. Stewart was recovering at home. When Merry wasn't with him, Garth was. I guess I got a little scared. She might not need me as much after Stewart got well. I pressured her. We—" He sprang up and ran to the window over the sink in the kitchen. "Where's Rosinna been?"

"Funeral arrangements, I guess," I said.

"That's rough about Stewart. It's weird how things work out sometimes. He goes for years on the booze. Never a scratch—except for his health. Then he falls down the stairs. Life doesn't make sense." He came back and fell into the armchair. "Anyway, Merry finally decided I was right. If we waited, Rosinna would find some way to break us up. So it was the day she disappeared that we drove into town and were married by a justice of the peace. I drove her back afterward so she could tell Stewart. I checked on an apartment for us. When I came back for her, Merry was gone. Everyone was so innocent. 'Oh my goodness! Where is Merry? Did anyone see her leave?' It made me sick! Rosinna was lying. I told her just what I thought of her. She ordered me off the place—said if I ever came back she'd have me arrested. I figured she really could so I stayed away, month after month, waiting. I was so sure Merry'd find a way to get in touch with me. Then sometimes I'd wonder. Maybe I pressured her too much. Maybe she wanted to be away."

"I don't think so," I said.

He shrugged and kept his face turned away. "I tried to find her."

"Garth's afraid she's..." I caught myself before I said more.

"She's not dead! They wouldn't have hurt her. She was the precious baby sister, the glowing debutante, Stewart's favorite. They've just got her stashed somewhere, a very exclusive private school. Maybe even a convent, for all I know. Merry's not dead!"

"We've got to talk to Rosinna."

"I'm ready!" Tom said. "I've been stupid to wait this long!"

"We can't ask her right out," I warned. "We've got to outsmart her, trip her up, and get her to tell us before she's realized what's she said."

"I'd like to know how you plan to do that!" He rubbed his hands together. "So far the only thing keeping me from killing her is the fact that she knows where Merry is. Otherwise..."

I climbed off the couch and hurried on ahead of him. He sounded okay, but I wasn't all that sure of what he might do. We went down to the tunnel. Tom felt for the light. "Wait a minute," he said. "Maybe I'd better get the marriage certificate. Maybe Rosinna never believed Merry. I need proof."

"Why wouldn't she have believed it?"

"You get her on the subject of what's proper and she goes haywire. If she doesn't want something to be, she just wills it away."

"I guess the only way we'll ever know is to ask," I said.

"Wait till I walk in. She'll come unglued. That's it! You go up first and I'll phone Garth again. I'll be right behind you."

With Tom's last words ringing in my ears, I turned, ready to tear up the kitchen stairs screaming Rosinna's name. I was halfway up when I realized that I didn't know what I was going to say. What would make her admit a secret she had guarded so long?

Rosinna sat hunched before the dying fire in the den with her face in her hands. She hadn't taken off her mink. She looked like a tragicomic figure, shaking with grief I wasn't sure she really felt. She looked up and hastily dashed away tears. "Merri, I looked all over for you. Forgive me, please. I just can't seem to stop crying. I can't believe Stewart's gone. My father—dead."

I sat down near her, my mind suddenly blank. Despite everything, I felt sorry for her. If ever Rosinna was at her weakest, it was then. I knew I had to take advantage of this one chance.

I hesitated. I wasn't the type to deliberately trick or hurt someone. This would be the end for Rosinna. Yet Rosinna hadn't hesitated, I thought. The day Merry came to her with the news of her marriage, Rosinna hadn't stopped to consider her sister's feelings. She'd acted—swept Merry so far away no one had been able to find her since. There was no time to feel sorry about the pain I might cause Rosinna. I had to get at the truth, and I was the only one that could do it.

"Everything's arranged," she said, flinging her hands up helplessly. "Awful—just awful. The funeral home was completely unsatisfactory, but there was nothing I could do. It would be highly improper to…Stewart mustn't be shuffled about simply because…" She pressed a thin fingertip to her lips as if to stop the flow of words. What else did she hold inside? I wondered.

"Jerome should have gone with you," I said.

"My poor brother. I told you how sensitive he is. He went straight to his room and hasn't come out. He's simply destroyed."

That was hard to believe. "Was he as worried after Merry disappeared?"

"Of course—devastated! Simply in pieces. That's what makes this so tragic. Stewart died without seeing Merry again. I tried, truly I did, to show him the kind of love Merry did, but it was never enough. I was too…impatient. I blame… myself for this horrible accident."

I couldn't tell if she really felt that way or if she was just feeling sorry for herself.

"My best was never worth anything," she cried. "Stewart had no use for me. I'm too much like my mother. He never loved Germaine. Consequently, he didn't love Jerome or myself nearly as much as he did Merry."

"Then when he made the arrangements for the estate and made his will…"

"It broke my heart. To be scorned by one's own father…"

"It must have made you awfully mad," I said. I leaned a little closer to see her expression. Did she realize where I was leading her?

"Jerome and I were just...crushed. Jerome didn't say a word, of course. He wouldn't dream of approaching Stewart about financial arrangements—much too dignified for that. Now Garth, he wasn't at all upset by the arrangement. He has his yearly retainer. On top of that, he got fifteen percent of the fortune—a mere stepbrother! All I wanted to know was what he was doing with our money. He carried on like... Garth is so cruel to me. Now, when I need him to arrange the funeral of the man who treated him like a son and made him wealthy, I cannot reach him. As usual I am powerless, a wellborn housekeeper. Merri, I feel so alone, so rejected. Of course, I understood that Stewart had the family to think of—Craggmoor, its future. If only—"

"You must have resented Merry," I said. "So young, yet entrusted with the estate's management." My heart beat faster and faster. Did she see what I was doing?

"It was so unfair. I'd hoped after Stewart got well he'd realize how he'd hurt Jerome and me, but..."

Slowly she raised her eyes. They flashed. Her lips formed an oval and she stood up, letting the mink slide to a heap on the couch behind her. "But I wouldn't...I wouldn't *dream* of asking my father to change his mind. If that was how he really wanted the estate divided...I respected Stewart! Regardless of my own feelings, it was his decision, his money. He was my father! You don't think..."

"I don't know what to think," I said, excitedly jumping up and facing her. "So many strange things have happened since I got here. Now Stewart..."

"What are you thinking!" she choked out, her face draining.

"You tell me."

"Garth has been feeding you his wretched theories, hasn't he?"

"Why shouldn't I believe Garth?" I said. "The very first day I was here you treated me like a criminal. Every chance you got you lied to me. That business about Merry running away…"

"You had no business knowing anything about my sister," she snapped.

"You lied to Garth, too."

"How I handled Garth is none of your business. I chose to spare him the coarse details and I would do it again. Leaving a fine home and devoted family—what was I to think of Merry?"

"Why lie?"

"You simply don't understand. I resent this inquisition."

"What really happened to Merry?"

"I don't know!" Rosinna cried. "Why does everyone insist that I do?"

"Because you talked to her last. You—"

"Stop it! I refuse to discuss it any further. I'm going to my room."

"No, Rosinna. Stewart died today because of you and your lies and the fact that someone tried to lock me up to keep me from finding out what happened to Merry. I think that 'someone' was you."

"Locked you up? Where? When?"

I ignored that. "Did you send her away?"

"Send her? Whatever for?"

"You can't go on lying forever. Tell me what happened. It's going to come out sooner or later."

"Really, Merri! You shock me!"

I glared at her. "If there's nothing to cover up, why are you trying so hard to keep me from finding Merry?"

"I've been perfectly cooperative!" She shook her head as if it hurt. "I've taken a complete stranger into my home and into my confidence. I have shown you the greatest courtesy. I had no idea you suspected me."

"I have ever since the first night when the prowler grabbed me. He was after you!"

Fear in her eyes betrayed her thoughts.

I glanced toward the kitchen. What was keeping Tom?

"You must believe me, I did nothing to her. I only tried to help. She was my sister. I wanted only the best for her," Rosinna said.

"Why do you keep hiding the truth then?"

"What *truth*?" she screamed.

"You hid that diary. Yes, I saw it!"

Her face went paler still.

"I don't know what was in it," I said with a triumphant smile, "but I can guess."

Rosinna was totally at a loss for words. She sputtered and gasped and finally fell back on the couch. "If I left that diary where you might have read it I was afraid you'd tell Stewart about her desire to marry that Tom person. Stewart would have been horrified. I protected him from the truth all this time. This is the thanks I get."

I sighed disgustedly. "It's no use. I know the truth."

Again she raised her eyes. "Then you know more than I. I did not make her go. She chose that course of action herself. I do not know where she went. She has not chosen to contact me. I have borne the burden of her heartlessness alone and watched my father suffer every day because of it."

"I don't believe you."

"Then you *do not* know the entire story."

She seemed to have gained control suddenly. It shook my confidence. Where was Tom? Had he deserted me? Even armed with the truth, I was no match for Rosinna's years of accumulated strength.

"I know about Tom," I said softly.

She put a trembling hand to her eyes and drew a deep breath. "Very well. I was only trying to protect her," Rosinna whispered. "You have no idea how destroyed Stewart would have been to learn Merry took up with the gardener, of all people."

"But they were in love!"

"Indeed? How would you know?"

"Because I talked to Tom."

She leaped up. "Merry's back?"

"No," I said, becoming thoroughly confused. "But Tom's here. He should have come up from the tunnel by now. We both want to know where Merry went. You're going to have to notify her of Stewart's death and there's no getting around that, is there? How can her marriage matter now that Stewart is dead?"

She shook a white-knuckled fist at me. "Don't you *hear* me? I do not know where Merry is! I thought she left to be with that worthless gardener and simply refused to be decent enough to write or call."

"You know she didn't. Tom came back for her and you sent him away. What happened to her?"

Rosinna burst into furious tears. "I don't know! I don't! I admit Merry and I argued. I was shocked that she'd marry a servant, but if it was her wish, I certainly didn't intend to interfere."

It was getting so darn hard not to believe her! If it wasn't the estate or the marriage that brought about the disappearance, what did then?

I was beginning to get dizzy. I squeezed my temples to blot out the pain of a growing headache. "Something is very wrong here," I said. "Someone knows where Merry is. Someone is trying to cover it up and is desperate enough to kill."

"Whatever do you mean?" she shot at me. "Are you accusing me of murder now, too?"

"I found Garth in the tool room this morning—unconscious! Someone hit him. Not an hour later someone pushed *me* into the furnace room and tied me up."

"Preposterous!"

"Deny it and I'll pretend it didn't happen either. Honestly, you almost convinced me. You're a terrific liar, Rosinna. You almost made me forget—I know Merry never left Craggmoor."

She stood slowly.

"I found her suitcase in the furnace room, locked in a cabinet. That was really careless. You could do better than that. Where is she? Are you keeping her prisoner somewhere?"

Rosinna just stood there, her composure in a shambles, her mouth hanging open, and tears rolling down her face. "I didn't! I didn't!"

My hair began to rise. She wasn't lying! She truly didn't know where Merry was!

"I think my sister needs rest," Jerome said unexpectedly from behind me. "Enough of this cruelty, Merri. Come away and leave Rosinna alone."

"Jerome," Rosinna sobbed, flinging herself against him. "Everyone thinks I, of all people, did something with Merry—my very own sister. Tell this mad young woman I had nothing but the best in mind for Merry."

"We *were* deeply fond of her," he said looking down at me from the height of his small head and scraggly neck. He moved stiffly from Rosinna, holding himself erect, his eyes pale as death, his mouth a grim crack in his pinched face. "Apologize to Rosinna."

I darted toward the door, but he caught me. His icy hand cut into my arm.

"Tell her you're sorry you made her cry. I do not tolerate persons who make my sister cry."

"Jerome, please, let her go," Rosinna sobbed. "She's overwrought because of Stewart's death. Her reaction is perfectly understandable. I forgive her completely."

"I will not allow anyone to make you unhappy," Jerome said calmly, his eyebrows lifted. "Only yesterday Garth made you cry. You nearly fell down the stairs. I hope he's learned his lesson."

"You tried to kill him!" I screamed.

"You are much too inquisitive for your own good," he remarked.

"You didn't!" Rosinna gasped. "You struck Garth?"

"He's had it coming for a long time."

"Did you push Stewart down the stairs?" I threw out recklessly.

"No!" he shouted, twisting my arm. "No! Don't you dare accuse me of that. Only Garth deserved to be punished. He isn't even a Glenden, so he has no right here."

168

"I can't believe it of you," Rosinna moaned.

I tugged to get free. "Where were you the day Merry disappeared?" I whispered.

Jerome's eyes jerked. He wrenched me around and pushed me ahead of him toward the entrance hall. His frigid calm was gone. He looked barely in control.

"Jerome, wait!" Rosinna wailed. "Where are you going?" She ran after him and pulled him around. "Let Merri go!"

"Don't stop me!" He flung her away.

Rosinna slipped, reached out to break her fall and cracked her head against the wall. She slumped to the floor, unconscious.

Jerome let me go and bent over her, his face crumpled. "I'm sorry! I didn't mean to hurt you."

"Tom!" I screamed, backing away. I pressed myself against the front door. "Florence! Tom! Somebody, help!"

Slowly, malevolently, Jerome rose. He turned to me. He smiled savagely. "They can't help you now."

I was sure I was going to faint.

Jerome started toward me. "I took care of them. Now I'm going to take care of you as I should have the minute you arrived. I'm going to show you what I do to girls who can't behave. I'm going to punish you the way I punished Merry. Then you'll say you're sorry. You'll see. You'll be so sorry you'll never speak improperly to my sister again."

Eight

Jerome's eyes gleamed with an unnatural fire. He looked like a crazed vulture, but just then I didn't have time to think about how funny it was. There was nothing funny about the way his fists clenched and unclenched or the way he bared his teeth.

"Help Rosinna," I said, pressing myself flat against the door.

Jerome waved her off as if she didn't matter.

"How could you hurt your sister?"

He paused long enough to look back at her and gulped sharply. With effort, he turned his attention back to me.

"Look at her! Don't leave her lying there like that, Jerry. Don't you love her?"

"Stop!" he shouted. "Don't call me Jerry. My name is Jerome Glenden." Then he lunged.

In panic, I threw open the front door and raced out into the cold. My feet plunged through bitter snow. It was only seconds before my fingers went numb. I paused by the

170

fountain and looked back. There he was, right behind me, running awkwardly, his grim face still set, his eyes spelling terror—maybe even death for me.

"I won't tell anyone I found the suitcase," I yelled, hoping maybe he'd give up and let me alone.

Jerome stumbled.

I dashed around the fountain and followed the drive toward the house, where it went alongside the ballroom. If I could get up to the highway, I might have a chance. Jerome cut across the hedges and drifts and was suddenly before me. His mouth hung open as he gasped for breath. His tongue hung out a little and suddenly I was so revolted I just bolted blindly.

I fell over a row of bushes, landing headfirst in the snow. Jerome seized me from behind and yanked me up. His fingers felt like claws of ice.

"Get going," he panted, jerking me tightly against him.

Each step I took was preceded by a jab in my back. He's crazy! He's really crazy, I kept thinking. I stumbled ahead of him, shivering and chattering. "I won't tell anyone!" I whispered hoarsely. I struggled and he ground his knuckles into my backbone.

"You're stupid," he muttered over my moan.

We followed the same path down past the cliff to the promenade. Jerome pushed me down the steps and marched me without stopping through snow almost a foot deep. My feet screamed with cold. My head ached. I couldn't seem to think any more. Vaguely I remembered ravines and jagged rocks hundreds of feet below the wall. Was that where Merry lay all this time, now just a scatter of bones under the snow? Would Jerome somehow finish me off there too? Would he make us snow sisters in death?

"You murdered Merry, didn't you?" I said through chattering teeth.

"No!"

"Merry and Rosinna argued. Did Rosinna cry? Is that why you…"

Jerome staggered over a drift. He veered off the promenade's path and began kicking around near the wall. "Merry always said cruel things to my sister—just like you did. Rosinna needs me to protect her."

"What are you doing?"

He held me by one wrist, but I couldn't pull free. I was beginning to shiver uncontrollably. Every movement I made was an effort. Jerome was too much for me.

"I'm so cold," I whimpered, feeling a stab of fear weaken me.

"You're going to get colder." He laughed, flicking his eyes over me with contempt. "She got cold, too."

Where he'd kicked away the snow his shoe caught on the edge of the drain grating. For a second he let me go. I just stood there, too cold to think or move. His face twitched as he heaved the grating to one side. The sounds he made suddenly frightened me so much I took a step away.

He whirled and smashed his fist against the side of my head. I went down half-conscious, half-blinded by the snow. When I rolled over, Jerome was half-crouched over the opening. I couldn't tell if he was laughing or crying. As soon as I tried to get up he leaped on me and dragged me toward the gaping black hole.

Don't, don't, don't! I thought. I felt dizzy and tired. I couldn't feel my fingers or get my legs to move as they should. "Don't," I mumbled.

"This is for your own good. When you've learned your lesson I'll let you out. If you yell I'll leave you in longer. It's cold down there, Merry. So you'd better be very good. You're going to stay in there until you promise never to make Rosinna cry again."

My legs slid over the edge. I threw out my arms wildly. They slapped against snow and ice. I couldn't grip the icy sides of the deep stone drain. Snow kept sifting into my eyes. I screamed. Jerome slapped me.

Rosinna's voice rang out. "Jerome!"

He let go. I wrapped my arms around his neck and hung on. We fell into the snow together. He threw me off with an infuriated roar and beat on my hands and struck my head.

"Jerome!" Rosinna called again, closer. "Jerome? Where are you?"

"Here!" I screamed. "Help!"

It was dark now, and it had started to snow. I saw the snowflakes through the trees as Jerome pushed me toward the hole again. He tried to stuff my flailing arms and legs into the drain. My shoe fell off and dropped, splashing some ten feet down. I felt myself slipping and couldn't get a good hold on anything.

The blinding beam of a flashlight cut across the promenade. It caught Jerome in the face and he ducked. I rolled away, feeling like a snowball, and pressed myself against the stone wall, hoping he wouldn't see me there.

"What are you doing?" Rosinna demanded, turning the flashlight on me, and then down the drain hole, and then back to Jerome. "My God! What are you doing?" Her voice shook and broke.

"I'll let her out in a little while. Then she'll be decent to you. I've got to teach her a lesson," Jerome said as if it were perfectly reasonable to attempt murder.

"You can't put her down there! She'll freeze!" Rosinna's shrill voice cracked with horror.

"No, she won't," he insisted. "She won't. I'll let her out later."

"You can't!" she cried. "You don't want her to die, do you? She hasn't done anything."

"She married that gardener, didn't she? She shamed the family. She made you cry. I heard what she said. You aren't jealous or spiteful. If you let me put her in the hole a while, she'll behave. You'd like that."

Rosinna stood perfectly still. The beam didn't waver. "How long will you leave her down there?" she asked softly, as if she was afraid her words might shatter a delicate balance.

"Until she promises—"

"Like you used to want Garth to promise when you locked him in the larder?"

"It would have worked if…You're too nice to people, but *I* know how to make them behave."

"But, Jerry…" she crooned.

"Don't call me that!"

"Jerome, this isn't our sister. Our sister is gone—gone two years."

"No, she's right down…" He shook his head. Then he laughed uneasily. "I'm your brother and I'm going to take care of you."

"You'll put her in that drain?" she asked lovingly.

"Then she won't upset Father and he won't drink or say unkind things to me. We have to stop Merry from causing so much trouble."

"How?"

"Just stop her!" Jerome exclaimed with exasperation. "I can't lock her up. The servants might see. This is so much better. It'll scare her! It's like solitary confinement."

"Jerry—Jerome," she wept. "You don't know what you're saying. This isn't our sister! We can't put her down there."

"I'll hit her. Then she won't scream. She *needs* to be punished."

"If you put her down there, you won't be able to get her out. Is that what happened before? You couldn't get her out? Was she already dead?"

He rubbed his eyes. "I'm going in now."

"Don't you dare look away from me!"

"I can't take her out till the gardener goes away. It's getting late." He shook his head. "If I don't hurry…" He started to cry. "I tried to let her out, Rosinna. Really I did! But I was…too late!"

The silent cold night settled around us like a shroud. I didn't dare speak for fear Jerome might realize that it was now, and not before when he put Merry in the drain to die.

Jerome went on sobbing. "I didn't intend for it to happen that way."

Rosinna's own sobs caught in her throat. The sound shattered the spell that had brought about Jerome's horrible confession. Slowly he raised himself up, tears no longer filling his evil eyes. "Don't *cry!*"

"How could you?"

His eyebrows went down and his mouth hardened. "She deserved it. She had everything—everything that should have been yours and mine. I'm not sorry! It's been better since…"

Rosinna burst into great sobs. The beam of her flashlight faltered. Jerome darted out of sight. He stumbled over me, and before I could fend him off, he jerked me to my feet and held me by the throat.

"Go in the house, Rosinna. We've kept it a secret all this time. We can keep it up for as long as we want. I'll be along in a moment. See? It's started to snow. Before long all the footprints will be covered, just like last time."

"You're insane!"

"Don't shout at me. You shouldn't be angry."

"I am very angry!" she cried. "Let Merri go. Now! I'm going to call the police."

"No, you won't." He shook me like a rag doll. I could hear his teeth grinding together.

His grip nearly choked me, but I was so stiff I couldn't fight him. He eased one leg over the wall and laughed when Rosinna let out an awful scream. Any minute both Jerome and I would plunge over the side. I couldn't even raise my arms to pull his fingers from my neck.

"If you don't go in the house…I'll jump," Jerome hissed.

"Get down from there. Please!"

She lunged forward and dropped the flashlight. We could hear her searching in the snow for it. The dim, snow-covered light let us see how terribly close she was getting to the yawning hole.

"Watch out!" Jerome yelled, dropping me.

Just as he tried to scramble down from the wall he must have lost his balance. It was so icy and dark. He must have been stiff too, too awkward and frightened to know what he was doing—and he no longer had my body to keep him from falling over the edge.

"It's deep!" Rosinna gasped.

Jerome threw out his arm. His shoes scuffed against the rocks. He struggled to get a handhold in the darkness. I heard a shuddering gasp—

Then his hideous scream rang out. Quietly his body plummeted to a snowy death on the rocks below.

For a moment all was death and silence. Rosinna lay nearby, taking in ragged breaths, one leg braced across the drain to keep her from dropping in. "Jerome?" She didn't seem to realize what had happened. "Jerome!"

I inched closer to her and put my hand out. When I touched her arm, she jumped. "Merri! I thought you went over with him." She seized me and dragged herself away from the hole. We huddled together for a moment catching our breath. My chest was beginning to hurt. The rest of me felt fine. I was either getting used to the cold or half dead.

The flashlight was still stuck light-down nearby. Rosinna snatched it up and dragged herself to her feet. She leaned over the edge of the wall.

"Careful," I whispered. "It's icy."

She turned suddenly and clutched the flashlight to her chest. It lit her face from under her chin, casting her eyes into shadows so black and tragic I would see them again in my nightmares.

At last she turned the light on me. "Are you hurt?"

I took her hand and got to my feet. They felt like stumps. The sudden pressure on them hurt more than if they had been sawed off. "I'm so cold," I cried, leaning against her. "My feet are frozen."

Rosinna leaned toward the hole and shined the light

down it. "I see your shoe," she said after a long time.

"Do you think…do you really think he put Merry… down *there*?"

She was coldly remote when she answered. "Jerome always did have emotional upsets. He couldn't attend ordinary schools and his tutors always said…But whatever he did, he did for me, out of love."

"You can't accept what he did!" I cried. "Jerome murdered your sister."

"No." She sighed. "I don't accept it. I didn't know about this. If I had…I loved my brother. It will hurt me deeply to have his name ruined." Again she shone the light down the drain. "I truly believed Merry ran off with the gardener."

I felt sick.

"You were wrong," she said. "I had no secrets to hide. I did nothing to prevent you from looking for your cousin, except hide her diary. Neither of us will ever invade the privacy of…"

"Stop it!"

"You can be so unkind."

"I like you better when you're screaming and hysterical. Then you're human, at least," I said, shuddering.

"That's uncalled for."

"I've tried to like you," I said. "But you're a phony and the way you're acting right now, after all that's happened, proves it."

She didn't answer. Slowly she sagged and began to weep again. "I'm not as self-assured and calm as you think. I do the best I can. If I'm wrong, then I'm sorry."

I was too tired to go on about it. "We've got to find Tom," I said. "And Florence. Jerome hurt them, too."

Rosinna wept more loudly. "Everything I've tried to build here is in ruin. Yes, let's go before I leap over that wall myself."

"We'll have to call the police."

"I know—I know. Craggmoor will be the target of public ridicule for..."

I shook her. "That's not important! If nobody cares about you, what difference does it make how you look to them? Stop acting like a robot and maybe someone could get to like you for yourself!"

"Please stop!"

"All right! Go ahead. Worry about the family's reputation. Imagine the embarrassing publicity, the scandalous stories. Then you won't have to think about the hell Merry went through the hours before she died."

Rosinna looked horrified. "If I think of that," she gasped, "I'll go mad!"

"Go ahead and think about it," came a voice from behind. "Think about freezing to death."

I didn't think I had enough strength left to feel scared again, but when I saw Tom standing in the darkness like a huge, angry shadow I did feel scared again—more scared than ever.

Rosinna aimed the flashlight at him, and, for a moment, we saw his face, an ugly mask of horror and grief. He lunged and tore the flashlight from Rosinna's hand. I watched, feeling like an ice sculpture, white, caked with snow, and numb through.

Rosinna looked almost as bad. Her hair looked like broken branches where it had mixed with her tears and frozen stiff.

"She's dead," he whispered. "Right?"

Rosinna threw her hands over her head and cried. "He didn't mean to let her die."

Tom seized her and shook her hard. "But he did! My wife has been dead all this time!"

Rosinna sobbed helplessly.

"Tom…" I said, suddenly very tired and beginning to sway. Their voices were drifting and for seconds at a time I couldn't hear them. "She didn't know."

He'd believed for so long that Rosinna was responsible, he just couldn't accept anything else. He kept shaking her until her head snapped back and forth. "I ought to throw you down there, too!"

Rosinna went limp. He dropped her like she'd suddenly stung his hands. Sanity came back into his eyes as he stared at her motionless body in the snow.

It all showed in his face, the pain, the shock. He let out a heartrending yell that pierced the darkness and sent my blood rushing like crushed glass through my veins. He sank to his knees beside the drain and jabbed the beam of light down it. "She can't be down there!" he shouted. "I don't see her. I don't believe it!"

The flashlight slipped from his hands and fell. It splashed quietly. I couldn't stand any longer. The snow looked soft as cotton. My mind blinked on and off like a light—light, dark, light. I put out my numbed hands and drifted forward. Waggling shafts of light came around the bend of the promenade, but once I was lying down, it didn't matter.

• • •

The touch of warm hands was painful. Someone lifted me up. My head lolled on a rough shoulder. Every movement caused pain, but I hung on. Voices, lights, blankets, warm hands—hot liquid scalded my throat. My body began to tingle with life. My skin turned to fire. I don't remember if I really screamed or not. I just know I wanted to.

The pain wasn't so bad when I finally woke up. Awkwardly, I tried to push back a crushing layer of blankets. Garth sat slumped on the edge of my bed rubbing the back of his neck. "How do you feel?" he whispered, leaning closer and taking one of my mitten-covered hands.

"Tired."

"You sure gave me a scare. The doctor says you'll be all right though. Can you move your toes?"

I tried one and that was enough to convince me I never wanted to move again. "Never!" I panted with my eyes smarting.

"Rosinna tried to tell us what happened." He cleared his throat. "The doctor had to sedate her. I've had a few stiff ones myself." His eyes did look a little glassy. I wanted to kiss him.

"You heard about Stewart?" I said, wondering why I was whispering.

He sighed with his whole body. Then he nodded.

My throat closed. Don't think about it, I told myself. Not now, anyway.

"There were half a dozen messages when I finally went home," Garth said, knowing I was wondering how he got back just in time. "Rosinna had called. The coroner had called. The messages were all the same: Stewart, Stewart, Stewart." With a shaky hand he rubbed his eyes. "Forgive me, Merri—I've been crying."

"It was my fault," I said, slowly easing up so I could reach him.

"Your fault!" he grunted. "He just fell."

"Someone locked me in the furnace room. I called Florence, but she didn't hear me. So I called Stewart. He thought…"

"Poor Florence has been tied up all evening, trussed up like a Thanksgiving turkey. She's mad as a hornet. She's downstairs fixing you more soup. Who locked you up? Jerry?"

I shrugged. "I guess. At least Stewart doesn't have to know. I have to admit I'm surprised. Rosinna never knew anything about Merry. There are only the two of you now. You'll have to work together to run Craggmoor."

"I've got all the luck. I'm sorry, Merri. You're right. Don't worry, I'll be nice to her. Never thought I'd feel sorry for her, but I do now."

"Is Jerry…dead?" I asked.

He nodded.

"And Merry?"

"Grisly, isn't it? To think we walked out there…" He cut himself off. "Senseless! My sister—frozen to death!"

"Don't think about it. The funeral will be bad enough."

"What about Tom?"

"He'll be okay. I won't press any charges." Garth took both my hands in his. "You never knew my sister, but you were the most important person in her life."

And now I'll never meet her, I thought. Somehow it felt like I'd lost a part of myself. "Where's Rosinna?" I asked after a heavy silence.

"Sleeping."

"I want to see her."

"She'd probably rather be alone."

"She's lost Jerome and Stewart...and Merry. She's got to have feelings even if she doesn't know how to show them. I think she's going to need us."

"I'll look in on her later."

"I said I want to see her, Garth. I'm okay now, almost."

"You are one hard woman to control!"

"I guess I am."

When I got up I felt almost too weak to stand. Garth put his arm around me and helped me down the hall. As we passed the open door of Stewart's room I stopped abruptly, blinked, and jerked back for a second look.

"What is it?"

I almost couldn't describe what caught my eye. "I thought I saw—oh, it's just a picture in my mind, a painting of Stewart by the window that I want to do someday. But...I could have sworn I saw...."

Garth hugged my shoulder as we went on to Rosinna's room. I didn't say anything more, but I felt sure I had seen someone in Stewart's room, a figure by the window—waving.

Garth knocked. Rosinna didn't answer. I pushed her door open anyway. Her room was dark. Garth switched on a nearby lamp.

"Please," she cried. "Leave me alone." She rolled over and pressed her face into her pillow.

I hobbled to her bedside and sank down beside her.

"Are you all right?"

"My father is dead. My sister's been murdered, two years in a horrible grave. And my brother's just killed himself. No! I am not all right. I'm sick and disgusted. Get out!"

"Come on, Merri," Garth muttered.

"Please go," Rosinna whispered. "I'd much prefer to do my crying in private."

"I'm sorry," I said, patting her awkwardly.

"For what?"

"For all my suspicions. For the terrible things I said. If I hadn't come here…"

"Stop being ridiculous, Merri. You saved us all from a… murderer. I guess I should get up and attend to things."

"It's all taken care of, Rosinna," Garth said quietly. "Don't worry about a thing. As soon as Florence has rested, I'm giving her a month off and enough money to go wherever she wants. Ah! Don't!" He smiled when she stared at him. "We'll manage alone, somehow."

I thanked him with my eyes. He shrugged sheepishly and looked wonderfully contrite. He came back to the bed then and bent down. His lips just brushed Rosinna's forehead. "I'm sorry, too. For all the times I——" He made a face and backed off. His neck got red.

"You needn't be so kind."

"I started a fire a while ago," Garth said. "Let's go down. It's better than lying around in the dark flogging ourselves over the past."

I got up with effort. "Will you come with us?"

She looked from me to Garth. I think for the first time I saw real happiness in her eyes.

"I'll be right down," she said, pushing back the covers.

Garth pulled me out of her room. As soon as he closed her door he spun me around and took me in his arms. His kiss took me by surprise. When he stopped I fell against him and gasped for breath.

"I think you're wonderful," he said. He kissed me again more slowly. "I shouldn't feel like this on the day of a tragedy, but darned if I don't. You're the loveliest girl I've ever known and I love you. After this is all over, I want to forget it ever happened. What do you want to do?"

I shrugged. "I haven't had time to think." I leaned against him and suddenly realized how free and safe I felt. Whatever had made Craggmoor forbidding and uncomfortable was now gone.

"Now that I know I'll never meet Merry—Garth, what *will* I do?"

"I don't know. All I know is that I want you to stay close to me—forever. I love you, Merri Glenden of Illinois. Don't ever go away."

On tiptoe, I reached his nose and kissed him lightly.

"I haven't shown you that ballroom yet, or the attic. You haven't read the journals or looked at the albums. I could tell you all about Merry—all the happy things."

My lips trailed along his cheek to his mouth. He seized me and held me tight. "Don't go away, please."

"Then, I won't," I said.

I knew the next days and weeks would be hard. Finding and losing Stewart and Merry so suddenly would not be easy for me. Yet now that it was over I could concentrate on a new purpose, a new consuming curiosity. What was Garth Favor like behind all his raw sarcasm and how soon would I become his wife?

As Garth and I started down the hall toward the warmth of the fire and savory soup waiting for us in the den, I said a silent thanks to my snow sister. Through her tragedy she had brought me to Craggmoor and her half-brother Garth.

I could almost see her walking up the snowy drive, smiling and waving. I could almost feel Stewart's joy in being with her again. I hope she approved of Garth and me. I knew we were going to be happy, so I think she did.

Hello, Merry, I thought, leaning against Garth's strong, warm arm. And good-bye.

CACTUS ROSE

In the heat of the southwest, desire is the kindling for two lost souls—and the flame of passion threatens to consume them both.

Rosie Saladay needs to get married—fast. The young widow needs help to protect her late husband's ranch, but no decent woman can live alone with a hired hand. With the wealthy Wesley Morris making a play for her land, Rosie needs a husband or she risks losing everything. So she hangs a sign at the local saloon: "Husband wanted. Apply inside. No conjugal rights."

Delmar Grant is a sucker for a damsel in distress, and even with Rosie's restrictions on "boots under her bed" stated firmly in black and white, something about the lovely widow's plea leaves him unable to turn away her proposal of marriage.

Though neither planned on falling in love, passion ignites between the unlikely couple. But their buried secrets—and enemies with both greed and a grudge—threaten to tear them apart. They'll discover this marriage of convenience may cost them more than they could have ever bargained for.

ANGEL

When her mother dies, fourteen-year-old Angel has no one to turn to but Dalt, a gruff-spoken mountain man with an unsettling leer and a dark past. Angel follows Dalt to the boomtowns of the Colorado territory, where she is thrust into the hardscrabble world of dancehalls, mining camps, and saloons.

From gold mines to gambling palaces, *Angel* tells the story of a girl navigating her way through life, as an orphan, a pioneer, and ultimately a miner's wife and respected madam…a story bound up with the tale of the one man in all the West who dared to love her.

AUTUMN BLAZE

Firemaker is a wild, golden-haired beauty who was taken from her home as a baby and raised by a Comanche tribe. Carter Machesney is the handsome Texas Ranger charged with finding her, and reacquainting her with the life she never really knew.

Though they speak in different tongues, the instant flare of passion between Firemaker and Carter is a language both can speak, and their love is one that bridges both worlds.

HURRICANE SWEEP

Hurricane Sweep spans three generations of women—three generations of strife, heartbreak, and determination.

Florie is a delicate Southern belle who must flee north to escape her family's cruelty, only to endure the torment of both harsh winters and a sadistic husband. Loraine, Florie's beautiful and impulsive daughter, bares her body to the wrong man, yet hides her heart from the right one. And Jolie, Florie's pampered granddaughter, finds herself in the center of the whirlwind of her family's secrets.

Each woman is caught in a bitter struggle between power and pride, searching for a love great enough to obliterate generations of buried dreams and broken hearts.

KISS OF GOLD

From England to an isolated Colorado mining town, Daisie Browning yearns to find her lost father—the last thing she expects to find is love. Until, stranded, robbed, and beset by swindlers, she reluctantly accepts the help of the handsome and rakish Tyler Reede, all the while resisting his advances.

But soon Daisie finds herself drawn to Tyler, and she'll discover that almost everything she's been looking for can be found in his passionate embrace.

SUMMERSEA

Betz Witherspoon isn't looking forward to the long, hot summer ahead. Stuck at a high-class resort with her feisty young charge, Betz only decides enduring her precocious heiress's mischief might be worth it when she meets the handsome and mysterious Adam Teague.

Stealing away to the resort's most secluded spots, the summer's heat pales against the blaze of passion between Betz and Adam. But Betz finds her scorching romance beginning to fizzle as puzzling events threaten the future of her charge. To survive the season, Betz will have to trust the enigmatic Adam…and her own heart.

SWEET WHISPERS

Seeking a new start, Sadie Evans settles in Warren Bluffs with hopes of leaving her past behind. She finds her fresh start in the small town, in her new home and new job, but also in the safe and passionate embrace of handsome deputy sheriff, Jim Warren.

But just when it seems as if Sadie's wish for a new life

has been granted, secrets she meant to keep buried forever return to haunt her. Once again, she's scorned by the very town she has come to love—so Sadie must pin her hopes on Jim Warren's heart turning out to be the only home she'll ever need.

TIMBERHILL

When Carolyn Adams Clure returns to her family estate, Timberhill, she's there to face her nightmares, solve the mystery of her parents' dark past, and clear her father's name once and for all. Almost upon arrival, however, she is swept up into a maelstrom of fear, intrigue, and, most alarmingly, love.

In a horrifying but intriguing development for Carolyn, cult-like events begin to unfold in her midst and, before long, she finds both her life and her heart at stake.

VANITY BLADE

Orphan daughter of a saloon singer, vivacious Mary Lousie Mackenzie grows up to be a famous singer herself, the beautiful gambling queen known as Vanity Blade. Leaving her home in Mississippi, Vanity travels a wayward path to Sacramento, where she rules her own gambling boat. Gamblers and con men barter in high stakes around her, but Vanity's heart remains back east, with her once carefree life and former love, Trance Holloway, a preacher's son.

Trying to reclaim a happiness she'd left behind long ago, Vanity returns to Mississippi to discover—and fight for—the love she thought she'd lost forever.